When I'm Loving You

Dedication

For anyone who needs a miracle;
May you have the love, faith, and hope to believe.

"Nothing is impossible with God."

Luke 1:37

Chapter One

Josiah Eastman rang the doorbell of 375 Westport Drive and waited for someone to come to the door. Gabe had told him not to come, but he was here anyway. Maybe Gabe would refuse to talk to him face to face, but Josiah had to follow God's leading. God had told him very clearly, 'Go see Gabe before you leave town,' and so he was here.

Mrs. Hanson opened the door and seemed surprised by his presence, meaning Gabe hadn't told anyone he might be stopping by. No surprise. But Gabe's mom was welcoming and invited him inside. Josiah stepped into the familiar foyer of the spacious and upscale home. It was the same but gave him a strange feeling, considering how much things had changed between him and Gabe in the last eighteen months.

"I think Gabe is in his room if you want to go on back," Mrs. Hanson said. "Is he expecting you?"

"Yes," Josiah said.

"Are you leaving for camp tomorrow?"

"Yes."

"I heard about you and Rachael getting engaged. Congratulations."

"Thank you," he said, accepting the hug she offered him. He knew she wished things could have turned out differently for Rachael and her son, but she also knew he wasn't the one to blame.

He turned toward the hallway and went to Gabe's room, knocking on the closed door and wondering if his presence would be ignored. But Gabe called out for him to come in, and he did.

Looking over his shoulder from where he was sitting at his desk playing a computer game, Gabe didn't look surprised nor thrilled it was him, and he said nothing. Josiah closed the door and crossed the room. Gabe's desk was in the corner by the window, and he could pretty much ignore him simply by not turning around.

"I told you not to come, dude."

"Yeah, well. I'm here."

Gabe remained silent, and Josiah waited. Waited for Gabe to turn around. Waited for the words he should speak to enter his mind. Waited for whatever God had told him to come here for.

Eventually Gabe turned around, leaned back in his computer chair, and folded his arms in front of his chest as if he preferred to get this over with. Josiah said what came into his head in that moment.

"You need to go see her, Gabe."

He rolled his eyes and turned around as if to end the conversation, but Gabe spoke with his back to him. "Why should I?"

"Because you should, and deep down you know it."

"It's pointless. I don't love her. I can't give her what she wants. It would be a complete waste of time."

"Have you tried?"

"Tried what?"

"Loving her?"

Gabe didn't answer that.

"Anything is possible with God," he said, not knowing where those words came from. He hadn't planned to say anything like that, but more words followed. "I know you don't think you can love her, but maybe you can. Just think for a minute how great that would be."

Gabe turned back around. "Great?"

"Yes, Gabe. Great. You loving the woman who is the mother of your child. You and Sienna being happy together. You being the dad that little girl needs. Brittany growing up with parents who love each other and give her brothers and sisters to grow up with. Giving her the life both you and I had. We take it for granted, but all of this—everything around you wouldn't be here if it wasn't for God's love for you, and your parents' love for each other. Can you imagine growing up without any of this?"

He didn't answer that.

"Love is a good thing, Gabe. If you know what's good for you, you'll give it a chance."

He waited for Gabe to speak, but when he didn't, he turned to leave. Gabe didn't stop him.

***

"What did he say?"

"Not much," Josiah said.

Rachael sighed over the phone. She felt hopeful earlier when Josiah called and said he was going to try and talk to Gabe one last time. But it didn't sound promising.

"You tried," she said, wanting to encourage Josiah and remind him he had always done his best in all of this. "And that was good what you said. When did you think of that?"

"While I was there. I think those were Jesus' words, not mine."

"It sounds like Him," she agreed, allowing a smile to come to her face. Maybe none of it would make a difference, but she took joy in the fact God hadn't given up. Maybe everyone else would, including her, and maybe they would have every reason to, but God wouldn't give up; she felt certain of that. He hadn't given up on her.

"I love you," she said. "I can't wait to see you tomorrow."

"I love you too. I should be there by one."

"I'll be ready. The whole summer together. Just think of it!"

"And a much better summer than last year—for both of us."

"Much, much better," she agreed. "That seems like a long time ago."

"Let's not break up or anything silly like that, okay?"

"Okay," she said. "I can handle that plan."

"And we'll keep hoping for the best for Gabe and Sienna."

"We can always hope," she agreed.

***

Sienna Johnson stepped into the backyard and took a deep breath of the cool evening air. She liked it staying light so late these days, and tonight she really needed an escape from the stuffy house. Brittany had been particularly fussy since dinner, and she didn't know why.

Walking to the hammock hanging between the two large maple trees along the west side of the yard and lying down, she stared up at the green leaves absorbing the setting-sun. Despite the difficult day, she had a unique feeling of peace. Earlier she'd left Brittany with her mom while she took a shower and cried. She tried to act strong about being a mom at nineteen, and she was a lot of the time. God was upholding her, but sometimes she lost it, and today had been one of those days. But lying here now with Brittany finally sleeping, she clung to the belief things would get better from here.

She wasn't exactly sure what she needed or wanted. In the past she thought she knew, but lately she'd been considering other possibilities besides Gabe changing his mind. That was her primary prayer, but God had other ways of meeting her needs. Her well-being, and Brittany's, wasn't dependent on Gabe Hanson. Maybe God would bring him back to her, or maybe He had someone else waiting in the wings.

"I believe, Jesus," she whispered. "I really do. I believe with You, all things are possible, and I'll just keep waiting to see what you have in mind. The form your grace takes, that's up to you. But to believe in it, that's up to me. And I do."

Chapter Two

Amber woke up feeling sick to her stomach. All week she had been telling herself everything was going to be okay. Nothing to worry about. She could have peace in seeing Elle again and trust Jesus to take care of her heart. But with the encounter only six hours away, she felt like none of this should be happening. She shouldn't be here, or Elle shouldn't be coming. She had always loved it here at Camp Laughing Water, but today she would rather be anyplace else.

She tried to go back to sleep. Dave had asked them to help with a food delivery that was coming today, but they had no need to be anywhere until then. Seth was still sleeping in the bed beside her, and on a normal morning she would have snuggled up next to him and fallen back asleep in his arms, but today her mind had too many anxious thoughts. She wanted to shut out the world, but she couldn't. This was going to happen whether she wanted it to or not.

Deciding to get up and go for a walk, she got out of bed quietly and dressed in the jeans and sweatshirt she had been wearing yesterday rather than getting something out of the drawers and waking Seth in the process. She felt the need to have some time by herself to think and pray. During the last two weeks, they hadn't talked about Elle coming except for yesterday when Seth had asked how she was feeling about it. She told him she wasn't sure, which had been true at the time, but now she felt like she *wasn't* okay and *couldn't* handle it. It was *too much* for anyone to expect her to deal with.

The calmness of the morning and the stillness of the lake made her feel better, as a good walk around the camp lake always did when she had heavy thoughts on her mind, but much of the anxiety remained. She could shut it out for the moment, but there was no stopping this day from taking place, and she couldn't fully release the worries and fears, just put them off for a few hours.

She knew she should pray, but she didn't know what to pray. She had been asking God to help her, but now that the day was here, she couldn't help but wonder how she ever agreed to this or why God would want to put her through it all over again. She was reminded of her tendency to have great faith before a particular moment came, but how that faith crumbled when the time arrived.

Ever since the day she married Seth, she'd been so full of optimism about their relationship and future together. They had a wonderful honeymoon at the beach, enjoyed carefree days with her family, and then got settled into their summer home earlier this week. All the while she felt her life couldn't be any more perfect. But that ended today, she felt certain. Reality was knocking, and she couldn't enjoy the nice view from the window any longer.

She wasn't too surprised when she saw Seth waiting for her on a bench overlooking the lake. Sleeping past eight o'clock was unusual for him, even when they'd been up late the night before. Yesterday they had gone to visit Ben and Hope, spent most of the day with her brother and his wife, returned to the camp, and then had private time together. She loved being with him. She was glad they had waited until they were married for physical intimacy, but she was also glad the waiting was over.

She went to sit beside him on the bench, and he pulled her close to him. "Good morning," he said, giving her a brief kiss. "You're up early."

"Not as early as I'll have to be starting next week."

"All the more reason to take advantage of today. You all right?"

She didn't answer that. She felt ashamed of her doubts and fears and didn't want to talk about it. What good would that do? Elle was coming today. If she didn't want to spend her summer here, she should have decided that before now.

He didn't force her to talk or tell her it was going to be okay, something she didn't think she wanted to hear, but then she felt annoyed when he didn't say anything. Feeling the anguish rising in her soul, she knew her happiness would come to a screeching halt today, and there was nothing she could do about it. She tried to hold the tears in, but she couldn't.

Seth held her tight, and he didn't have to ask to know what was wrong. She wondered how he was feeling and realized she'd never asked him last night when they talked about it, but she knew all of this affected him too. He had kept things from her last summer regarding Elle's behavior toward him, and he felt horrible about it. Elle had told lies that hurt her deeply, but Seth had kept the truth from her and hurt her in a different way, something she didn't blame him for. But he blamed himself.

Remembering whom she was with, Amber lifted her face from Seth's warm neck and found his sweet lips. She wasn't alone in this. Seth would take care of her like he'd promised, and she needed to believe it and take care of him too. She felt certain assuring him of her love and forgiveness was the best way she could do that.

"I know it's going to be okay," she said. "I'm always okay with you."

***

Gabe woke up with Sienna on his mind. Lying there for a long time, he thought about what Josiah had said to him last night. They both had been home from college for a month, but Gabe had only seen his former best friend twice. Once three weeks ago and then again yesterday.

He wasn't sure why Josiah's words had stuck with him this time, but they had. And the truth was he'd been thinking about calling Sienna, just to appease her dad if nothing else. Mr. Johnson had been over here one day last week, ranting and raving about his lack of manhood and not taking responsibility for his choices.

Why did everyone see this as his fault? Sienna was the one who had lied to him about being on birth control, and maybe he shouldn't have been sleeping with her, but she'd been very willing. He hadn't had to talk her into anything, and she was the one to talk him into staying that first time and couldn't keep her hands off him after that. He enjoyed the pleasure of sex, but he never loved her. Why should he start now just because she had his baby? Even if he made the effort, he was certain it wouldn't last.

But this morning he woke with a different mindset. Maybe he could try. If he tried and it didn't work, he could tell people that, and then maybe everyone would leave him alone.

Getting out of bed and taking his phone from his desk, he decided to make the call before he changed his mind. He hadn't talked to Sienna in six months. After learning she was pregnant, he kept seeing her until he left for school, called her a few times from his dorm room, and saw her at Thanksgiving; but before he went back to school for the last few weeks until Winter Break, he told her it was over. She wanted to get married; he didn't. She wanted to keep the baby; he didn't want her to. She called him a couple of times after that, but when he told her he'd made up his mind and there was no changing it, she left him alone.

When she had the baby in March, she let him hear about it through others. After he returned home last month, she hadn't called and asked him to come see her. That confused him. Leaving him completely alone for six months, especially in her needy position? At first he thought she'd found someone else to love her, but no one had mentioned another boyfriend, not even a temporary one.

He called her cell phone like he always had when they'd been seeing each other secretly, and she answered.

"Hello?" she said. He could hear the apprehension in her voice. Her phone was telling her it was him, but she didn't believe it yet.

"Hey, Sienna. It's Gabe."

"Hi," she said in a voice he wasn't used to. She sounded different than he was expecting. More sweet and calm than he remembered.

"Is this a bad time?" he asked.

"No, this is fine. How are you?"

"I'm okay. How are you?"

"I'm good," she said, not sounding overly cheerful like she was faking happiness, but not like she was returning a formal greeting either. He got the feeling serious changes had taken place since he last talked to her. Again he wondered if she'd met someone else and her new boyfriend was the reason for the settled tone in her voice.

"Why are you calling me?" she asked, again sounding straightforward. She wasn't mad or had any particular expectations, but she needed to know what this was about.

He almost said, 'Because Josiah's making me', but that wasn't true, and he knew such a comment wouldn't be for the best, so he said what he'd been thinking for the past twenty minutes.

"Could you meet me somewhere today? Just to talk?"

"Yeah, maybe," she said, sounding more guarded.

"If you'd rather not, it's fine. I'm not trying to cause trouble for you or play games, or have any particular intentions. I just feel like we should talk. Maybe hear things directly from you about what you think of me instead of from everyone else."

"Like who?"

"Josiah, my mom and dad, your dad—"

"My dad?"

"He paid me a little visit last week. You didn't know?"

"No," she said. "I'm sorry, Gabe. If that's why you're calling—I don't want you to see me because you feel forced to. I know this was my fault. I've accepted that, and I'm done blaming you. I'm sorry if others are giving you a hard time."

Gabe was stunned by her words. *Who is this person? This isn't the Sienna I know.*

He felt very satisfied for a moment, like 'Thank you, finally! The truth is out. Why couldn't she be saying this to everyone else?' But remembering Josiah's words that had led him to call her, not because he was looking for an apology, he thought about what he should say. He had called to explore the remote possibility he could love her. And nothing in the conversation so far gave him a reason to disregard it.

"I'd still like to see you," he said. "Just to talk. If you want."

Chapter Three

Sienna didn't know what to say. She wanted to see Gabe, but she didn't know if she could go there. About a month before Brittany was born, she'd accepted the reality that Gabe had never loved her, admitted the truth to one of her close friends that getting pregnant had been more her fault than Gabe's, and put her complete trust in Jesus to lead her on from there. And she'd been doing all right. It had been a slow healing process, she'd felt incredibly alone at times, and she still had her tough days. But Jesus was carrying her, and she had allowed herself to hope that someday she would be loved simply for who she was, not for what she gave to a guy, and that her daughter would have a good father who wanted to be in their lives.

She'd lived in a world of 'If Onlys' for a long time. 'If only Gabe would love me instead of Rachael. If only he'd sleep with me, then he would stop thinking about her. If only he would marry me and take care of me and this baby, then my life would be perfect. If only...' the list went on and on. And not just with Gabe, but with expectations she had of her family and friends, her teachers, her bosses, and her other boyfriends in the past.

"Could I pray about it and get back to you?" she said.

"Sure," he said, sounding surprised she would say that, and she knew why. That wasn't like her. She wasn't the Sienna he used to know. "It doesn't have to be today," he added. "I'm here until the end of August, so whenever."

She laughed. "I'll try to get back to you before then. I really do appreciate you calling, Gabe. I just need to think. A lot has changed since I last talked to you."

"Are you seeing someone else?" he asked.

"No."

"Okay. I'll just wait to hear from you then."

Telling Gabe good-bye for now and clicking off her phone, she did take a moment to pray until she heard Brittany crying from the other room. She knew it was time to feed her again, not giving her a chance to think further until she was feeding Brittany ten minutes later.

Gabe called. She kept thinking that over and over. She hadn't necessarily prayed for that or been hoping for it, but now that it had happened, she knew if there was even a remote possibility of Gabe truly falling in love with her and wanting this, then she did too.

But the question was, did that possibility exist? Is that why he had called, to reconsider their relationship, or was he feeling guilty and felt like he had to? She didn't want that. She'd been down that road with him already, and trying to hang on to someone who didn't want to be hung on to was exhausting, unfulfilling, and had only left her with a broken heart and a baby to care for on her own.

***

Kerri wasn't feeling terribly stressed about her wedding coming up one week from today, but she had a lot to do. She was going shopping with her mom and older sister in an hour, and looking over her remaining to-do list, she tried to plan out an itinerary of their day. It was mostly a lot of little things, and the only thing she had a specific time to be somewhere was for her final fitting of her dress. They were due at the boutique in downtown Portland at eleven.

She would've had a lot of the other things done by now if she had been in town, but she hadn't. Following her brother's wedding, she had returned to California with Kevin, spent the week with him and his family, attended Jenna's wedding last weekend, and only returned home on Monday. Kevin wasn't coming until Wednesday of next week, and she thought she would have plenty of time to pull all the last-minute details together. She wasn't feeling any different about that now, but waking up this morning, the reality hit her: 'I'm getting married next Saturday. Am I ready? This is the rest of my life I'm talking about. I'm only nineteen. Am I being completely crazy?'

She took comfort in the fact her older sister had gotten married at nineteen too, and her twin brother had married Amber two weeks ago. But somehow she'd always imagined taking more time going from being a high school student to an official adult. She had envisioned those nebulous years of her late teens and early twenties where she was going to school and enjoying life and being dependent on her family and independent from them at the same time.

She'd imagined moments of certainty and uncertainty in her dating life, career plans, and future. She had imagined hanging out with her girlfriends, spending Friday nights with her boyfriend, balancing her time between family, friends, and activities. She imagined going to school for nine months out of the year and spending her summers as a carefree college student, working at camp, going on a mission trip or two, having traveling adventures, and even doing the unexpected—something she didn't plan in advance; but she'd never imagined this.

Kevin was her best friend. She had other friends, both girls and guys, but if she had the choice between spending time with Kevin or anyone else, he would win every time. She wasn't spending this summer with any of her other friends, or even her family. She was spending it all with Kevin: six weeks in Alaska and a few weeks back in California before starting her sophomore year of college. She wouldn't be living in the dorm or living on campus. She would be sharing an apartment with her husband in town and commuting to school every day.

She knew it was what she wanted, even if she couldn't fully picture it all in her mind. She expected to be happy. She knew God was leading her in this, and she was following. She had peace about it, and her joy was overflowing. She'd only been away from Kevin for five days, but she missed him already. She couldn't wait until he got here and for next Saturday to come, and yet in the back of her mind she wondered if it was all going to be as great as she was anticipating.

What if she missed her family too much this summer? What if being married to Kevin was a lot different than their relationship had been thus far? What if she married Kevin next Saturday and then woke up on Sunday saying, 'What have I done? I'm not ready for this. What was I thinking?'

Feeling the most unsettled she had all week, she decided to call him before tackling this day. He wouldn't be working until this afternoon, and she caught him at home. She had called him several times this week. He seemed to be doing all right with Jenna being gone, although he had confessed not liking being there at night all alone. He'd never lived alone, and the few times in the past when his sister had been out of town, he always spent the night at his parents' house, but he decided to try this week on his own, and he'd made it through the week, but he didn't like it.

"Good morning," she said. "How's my favorite fiancé today?"

"Kerri, I'm your only fiancé."

"Oh, that's right. How's my *only* fiancé?"

"Fine," he said.

"How did you sleep?"

"Okay. I got home late last night, and I was tired."

"I wasn't. I couldn't sleep. I kept thinking about you and wishing you were here."

"I wish I was. I miss you, Kerri."

"I miss you," she said and then asked him something on a whim. She knew Kevin might not want to change his plans. He could be very "stuck in his plan" sometimes, and she would be okay if he was, but it was worth a shot. "Do you think maybe you could come tomorrow instead of waiting until Wednesday?"

"Can I come today?" he asked.

She laughed. "Yes, I'd love that. But can you? Are you packed?"

"Mostly. I have a few things I need to buy for Alaska, but I can get them up there."

"I love you, Kevin. And I love the way you love me."

"I love you too, Kerri. See you soon."

***

Michaela Forester was excited about today, and a little scared. She'd been working at camp for the past three summers, and she loved everything about it. But going to a new camp she wasn't as familiar with made her wonder how different it would be, and taking on a leadership role was bound to be a challenge.

But she thrived on challenge. She always had. And that's why she had decided to go to Camp Laughing Water this year. At Cedar Creek they didn't allow anyone under twenty to be in a leadership position, but she was ready now and had felt God leading her to make the switch. She had been to Camp Laughing Water several times as a camper. The only reason she started going to Cedar Creek following her eighth-grade year was because the Christian camp also had a sports emphasis. Campers could choose from volleyball, basketball, soccer, swimming, diving, and water polo, and it was similar to going to a sports camp except there was the spiritual emphasis as well as an athletic one.

She played volleyball, basketball, and soccer and had been on her high school teams in those sports along with summer leagues. She had played soccer at Lifegate this year. She didn't consider herself to be a super-competitive person. She played more for the enjoyment of it and the personal challenge than for a winning season, but they had ended with a good record this year, and she was looking forward to getting back to it in the fall.

But for now, sports would have little to do with her summer. She was going to be in charge of the girl counselors, and her role would be a people-focused one rather than activity-based. She was excited and felt she had the leadership skills to fill the role, but she also knew a lot of emotions could come into play she wasn't as good at dealing with. She had a steady personality, rarely let emotionally-charged situations distract her from living her even-tempered life, and she could get frustrated with others easily who were the opposite of that.

When she had originally been thinking of going to Laughing Water this summer, she thought she would have Kerri here too. Kerri was a lot like her, and they got along well because of it. Kerri wasn't driven by her emotions either, and knowing she would have at least one stable-minded counselor under her, as well as having Kerri for a friend, she knew that would be a tremendous asset. But now Kerri wasn't going to be here. She had gotten to know a few of the girls this year at school who would be at camp too, but she didn't know any of them well enough to know exactly how she would get along with them in this setting.

The person she was most looking forward to getting to know better was Amber. She'd heard a lot about her from Kerri and had seen it for herself this year at school. She knew for Amber to have gotten Seth's attention, let alone marry him, she had to be a very special person, but Michaela wasn't too sure how much time she would have with her. They would be working separately a lot of the time, and she could imagine Amber wanting to spend any free time she had with Seth, rather than some girl she didn't really know.

And then there was this whole thing with Elle to deal with she wasn't looking forward to. Being around girls on emotional-overload was one thing, but being around someone who was manipulative, dishonest, and unpredictable was quite another. She'd been burned by someone like that a couple of years ago. Someone she had trusted and never would have imagined turning on her like she did, and it had been difficult to be completely open and vulnerable with others since then. She wanted to trust people and think the best of them, but sometimes her guard went up and she kept new people at arm's length. Trusting someone known to be untrustworthy would be all the more difficult.

But if she had learned anything about herself in the last nineteen years, she knew she thrived on challenge. When her parents had divorced at the age of eleven, it had made her stronger. When her friend had betrayed her during her junior year, she'd learned the value of true friends. When she had been denied several athletic scholarships, she accepted the one for a smaller school, but Lifegate had turned out to be a great decision. She might be going to a school that didn't put a lot of emphasis on competition and athletic success like she'd been used to for a long time, but she needed that. She needed to have her focus on God, not the achievements of life, and her year at Lifegate had helped her in that.

Arriving at the camp at eleven, she went looking for someone—anyone. There were a couple of cars in the parking lot and an older truck parked in front of the large building she was headed toward, but otherwise the place looked deserted. She knew she was a little early, but someone had to be here.

Stepping into the large cafeteria, she could hear voices coming from the kitchen area, and she wandered to the open window between the large room and the food prep area.

"Hello?" she called out when she could still hear voices but saw no one.

A face appeared from behind a workspace blocked by large freezers, and she smiled. Someone she knew, yea!

"Hi, Michaela," Seth said. "You made it."

"I did," she said. "I'm a little early."

"Dave will love that," he said.

"Is that Amber with you?"

"It is," he said. "Come on back and say hello. She's trying to find some marshmallows."

"For s'mores?" she asked, stepping through the doorway and walking toward Seth.

"No, for something we're doing later."

"Found some," she heard Amber say before she saw her. Amber was standing on the counter, holding the marshmallow bag in her hand.

"Hi, Amber," she said. "Mission accomplished, huh?"

"Yep," she said, flashing her classic smile and handing the bag to Seth before she climbed down from her high perch.

"She can find anything," Seth said.

Michaela stepped closer to give him a hug. She had known him forever, and it was good to have a familiar face to connect with during her first few minutes.

"Including the perfect husband," she said, referring to his words about Amber being able to find anything. "Congratulations. I heard from Kerri it was a perfect wedding."

"It was pretty nice," Seth said, reaching for Amber's hand and pulling her close to his side. They were so sweet together. She'd always thought so, but especially now. She envied them; not that she was jealous or wished she could have Seth for herself, but she wanted what they had—real love with the right person.

"I'm looking forward to working with both of you this summer," she said. "I was so excited when I found out you were going to be here."

"Do you want to get settled in your room?" Seth asked. "We can show you where it is."

"Sure. Lead the way."

They both stepped toward the back door of the kitchen, and she followed them. Her car was parked on this side of the building, and her room was just up the path. They helped her with carrying her things, and before she knew it she was entering her home for the summer. It was small, but clean, and there were two beds in the room.

"Who will I be sharing with?" she asked. "Do you know?"

"Not Amber," Seth joked. "She's with me."

"Yes, I know, Seth Kirkwood."

"I'm not sure," he said seriously. "What do you think, sweetheart? Megan is on the program team this year, but she'll be with Justin. I think the rest of the senior staff are guys, aren't they?"

"Yeah, I think so," she said. "It might be just you."

"Fine with me," she said. "After living with three girls all year, I can use the solitude."

Chapter Four

Arriving at Jessica's house before noon, Chad knocked on the front door and waited for someone to open it. He was coming to take Jessie to lunch and planned to spend most of the afternoon with her. She had gone up to Washington with her family this week, and he'd missed her. He also missed not being headed for camp today when he knew the rest of the summer staff would be doing so.

She opened the door and greeted him with a smile and an 'I missed you' hug. He was a little surprised at her clinginess, as if she hadn't seen him for months instead of only a week, but he didn't mind. He felt the same way.

"Welcome back," he said. "I missed you."

"I missed you," she said.

He hadn't planned to but kissed her right there in the open doorway for a long time. No one else seemed to be around, and Jessie didn't mind his extended stay. She was only returning the gentle affection, but it made him feel things in a hurry. He let out a soft groan and pulled away from her reluctantly. "If no one else is here, don't tell me that."

She smiled. "Daniel is. Let me go tell him I'm leaving, and we can go."

They both stepped inside, and he waited by the door for her to go upstairs and find her brother. Standing there in the grand foyer of the large house, he was reminded of why he couldn't marry her yet. *I'm never going to be able to provide for her like this. Even if I graduate and become a pastor, pastors don't make this kind of money. Maybe I should switch majors. I could do something in computers, or business, or even go to medical school if I set my mind to it.*

"Okay, we can go," Jessie said, coming down the stairs and taking her purse from a table in the foyer. He opened the door and followed her out, and he made a vow to himself to keep his kissing to a minimum.

He didn't have a lot of extra spending money, but he had enough to treat her to lunch and a matinee movie, and he did. He was working this summer, but he needed to save as much of it as possible for school. He'd been given a one-time monetary scholarship from his high school that had covered half of his expenses last year that grants didn't cover, so between that and his job at Tony's he hadn't had to borrow any money yet, and he wanted to keep it that way if possible. He wouldn't have that scholarship money this year, so his summer earnings would have to be enough.

He could have worked today and gotten some overtime, but he needed time with Jessie too. They had only planned on spending the afternoon together, but when she invited him to stay for dinner with her family, he couldn't refuse. If he had a choice between having time with Jessica and being somewhere else, she would win every time.

***

Elissa Rasmussen gave her dad a hug, and he told her to drive safe. "I will," she said. "And I'll be home in two weeks for the wedding."

"Have a good time."

"Thanks, Dad," she said. "I'm sure I will. Camp is always a good place to be."

She got into the car and selected music to listen to before pulling out of the driveway and waving good-bye to her dad. One of the most difficult things she'd ever had to do was leave him standing there last fall when she left for college in California. Her mom had died the previous summer, and with her older brother away in the Marines, she had left him all alone for the first time.

She almost hadn't gone, but he insisted she get away from home like she'd always planned on doing for college, and going to a smaller private college had always appealed to her more than a big state university. He'd known that and had been supportive of her plans. He had always been that way in everything else too, but leaving him alone had been more difficult than she'd anticipated beforehand.

She knew it had been for the best now. He'd met another woman this winter while she had been away at school, and they were getting married in two weeks. Elissa wasn't sure it would have happened if she hadn't been gone. Maybe, but she could imagine her dad being more reluctant to spend time with other women if she had been around. She liked Gina and was fine with her dad getting remarried, and she'd told him so several times, but he seemed cautious about it, like he didn't want her to see it as forgetting about her mom.

But Elissa didn't see it that way. She saw it as her dad being lonely and needing someone to share his life with again. Her mom and dad had gotten married when they were nineteen, been dating for two years before that, and been together for almost twenty-five years. She knew her dad had loved her mom very much and losing her had been a great loss. She didn't expect him to remain alone for the rest of his life.

She had decided to go to camp this summer when she heard they were getting married. She knew her dad and Gina would be fine with her being home, but she felt the need to give them time alone for now. Maybe next year she would come home for the summer and they could be like a family then, but for now she thought it would be awkward—for everyone.

Driving through the mountain highway in central Oregon toward the Willamette Valley, she had mixed feelings about going to camp too. As far as her dad knew, she was nothing but excited about it, but in reality she wasn't sure what to expect or how great it would be. She had worked at the camp three summers ago, and it had been okay. Initially she'd been excited about being away from home for the first time, but relationship issues had made for a long summer.

She had liked several different guys, but none of them had returned the interest. Her best friend, Abby, had a date just about every weekend, and she usually tagged along or was set up with another guy, but she never had a very good time. She and Abby had been best friends since the fourth grade, but they were very different, and Elissa had often felt inferior to her, but especially that summer.

On the one hand she wished Abby was going to be there this year, but on the other she was glad she wasn't. They had been roommates at college this year, and it had been okay. Most of the time they'd been too busy with their individual classes and homework and on-campus jobs to spend a lot of time together, and she managed to finally find a steady boyfriend, so it wasn't like Abby was always going out and leaving her, or making her tag along on her dates with whomever her boyfriend-of-the-month was.

She and Cory had been together for seven months now, but she hadn't seen him for the last three weeks, and she wouldn't be seeing him until August. He lived in southern California, and she'd gone there for a week to meet his family after the semester had ended, but then he left to go on a backpacking trip through Europe, and he wouldn't be back until two weeks before school started again.

He was sweet, and she felt like they had a good relationship, but she didn't know if she was in love with him. He was serious and studious, and they spent their time together doing homework or talking, more so than hanging out and having fun. She liked spending time with him, but they didn't have a lot in common other than being college students. He didn't even go to her school. He was a year older than her and a student at Humboldt University.

Arriving at the camp an hour after leaving home, she parked her car in the small lot by the dining hall and followed the staff registration signs pointing inside the building. She was expecting people she knew to be here. No one she was especially close to, but she knew of some from Lifegate, and she suspected there may be a few others from three summers ago. She didn't know that for sure, but Camp Laughing Water was one of those places many of the same people returned to year after year, first as campers, and then as returning staff. If her mom hadn't gotten sick, she likely would have been one of them.

***

Amber and Seth took the first shift of the two-hour staff registration time. Amber felt anxious about Elle possibly arriving during the hour, but she quickly got into the routine and joy of welcoming other staff members as they streamed in at an even pace.

There were early-birds who were already lined up outside the door before one o'clock, but otherwise they trickled in one after the other—some who were barely sixteen and very excited about being here, others who were also new but a little older and more "mature" about embarking on their summer experience, and then of course there were the veterans both Amber and Seth were happy to see again.

Matt and Mandy arrived at one-thirty, and Amber felt calmed by her cousin's presence and giddy about both her and Matt being here. She knew spending the summer with them would be very fun.

"How was the honeymoon?" Matt asked.

"How do you think?" Seth shot back.

They all laughed, and Matt pulled Mandy close to him and gave her a light kiss. "We'll be finding out about that real soon, won't we?"

"Hey, now," Seth said. "No kissing here, Spider-Boy."

"Oh yeah, sorry," he said, not looking too sorry about it. "It might take me a few days to get used to that."

Matt and Mandy both took their staff shirts, and they sent them on their way to find their rooms and get unpacked. "We'll be up there around two," Seth said. "We'll let you know what your first assignment is then."

"Oh, man," Matt said. "You don't expect us to actually work this summer, do you?"

"Not unless you want to be a counselor and never see your fiancée."

"Okay, I guess it's a small price to pay," Matt said, giving Mandy another kiss, but catching himself this time. "Oops, sorry, Nemo. Go easy on me. She's too beautiful to just stop cold turkey."

After they were gone, Seth turned to her and smiled. "Can't say I blame him," he said, giving her a kiss. They were alone for the moment, and kissing wasn't against the rules for married couples. He followed up his kiss with concerned words. "Are you doing all right?"

"Yes," she said. "Meeting everyone is reminding me of why I wanted to be here."

"Me too."

They continued with greeting those who arrived during the next half-hour, and Amber let out a little sigh of relief when they were replaced by Blake and Michaela. They'd made it through the first hour without having to face Elle. Amber knew they would be seeing her at some point today, but now it wouldn't be in such a face-to-face way.

Before going to meet Matt and Mandy and giving assignments to those on crew staff who had already arrived, Seth led her up to their room for a few minutes of privacy. Since arriving earlier this week, and every day since their wedding, they'd become used to showing their affection to one another freely, and having to hold back somewhat hadn't settled too well with Seth apparently, because he seemed very needy once they were alone, and he wasn't afraid to show it.

"This is going to be a tough summer for me, Amber."

"Why? I'd think it would be the easiest," she laughed. "You get to work with me every day and do this whenever we can find the time."

"I don't mean that," he said. "I mean having to take care of you. I love you so much, and the thought of you being in a difficult situation stresses me out."

She appreciated his concern, but she knew he couldn't spend his summer feeling that way. Giving him a hug, she told him something she believed with all of her heart, even if it was difficult to believe today.

"Jesus is going to take care of me, Seth. Let Him carry me, okay?"

"I'm trying, but it's tough, baby."

He held her for a moment and then commented on something that had happened earlier. He hadn't said anything about it at the time, and she hadn't expected him to, but she wasn't surprised when he did now.

"Is having Michaela here going to be difficult for you too?"

"No," she answered quickly. "I know she's not like Elle, and I'm not worried now that I know how you see her. I just let my imagination run away with me on that."

"So everything's okay? You're doing okay today, really?"

"Yes. I was hoping we wouldn't have to see Elle right away, and we didn't. That makes me feel like Jesus already has it covered. I really don't have to worry about this. I just need to trust Him."

Chapter Five

Elle O'Brien put her last bag into the car and hoped this wasn't a mistake. She'd made enough of those in the past two years. Mistakes that had hurt others and herself. Mistakes she didn't deserve to be forgiven of, and yet she knew she was.

I ran from you, God. Why didn't you let me keep running? Why did you have to come after me?

She'd asked the questions a dozen or more times since receiving her acceptance letter to be a part of the staff at Camp Laughing Water. She only applied because of Nick. He had talked her into it, and she only gave in because she didn't expect to be asked to come back.

I can't face those people again. What am I doing? She would have broken into tears if she didn't need to get on the road. She needed to pick up Nick, and she didn't want to make him late too.

Going inside the house to say good-bye to her mom and dad, Elle put on her happy and excited face, telling them good-bye and saying they didn't need to worry about her going off to camp for the summer. When she returned last year one week after leaving, she told them she wasn't ready to be away from home like that. But now, after being away at school this year, she was okay.

She found it ironic that last year she'd been more anxious to get out of here than this year, but she was acting like it was the opposite. She had been trying to be honest with people the last few months, but letting her mom and dad in on all of her failures seemed like too much.

She couldn't tell them she felt apprehensive about going because she would have to tell them why, and she couldn't bear the thought of the look on their faces when she told them what a horrible thing she had done. Some of her other mistakes they would likely excuse away as being part of learning things the hard way sometimes, but what she had done to Seth and Amber was inexcusable. If she had a daughter who had done such a thing and she found out about it, she would disown her.

On the drive to Nick's house, she had one thought that kept running through her mind. *Amber and Seth hate me. They are going to hate that I'm there. And everyone who knows them is going to hate me too.*

Her negative thoughts subsided somewhat after picking up Nick and journeying down the highway with him. He never allowed her to wallow in depression, suffocate in anxiety, or think too little of herself. He was the best friend she'd ever had.

She couldn't believe she had known him less than six months. He felt more like a brother she'd known her whole life. And even though he'd changed a lot since first meeting him, one thing hadn't changed: their honest and comfortable connection with each other.

He was another source of irony for her. All those years of inviting her friends to church and preaching at others who wouldn't come, with very little fruit to show for it, and then when she decided to give up trying to follow God, let alone lead anyone to Him, along comes Nick: a very lost and troubled soul who was so starved for love it had only taken one simple conversation about God to convince him he needed Jesus. And in the months since then, he'd been completely transformed right before her eyes. And she had been transformed in the process.

Living within an hour of the camp, they were pulling into the gravel driveway before she knew it, and the numb feeling she had been carrying around all morning led her to the registration area and into the building where she knew she might be facing Amber and Seth in a matter of seconds. But two other people were sitting at the table instead. One she knew, and one she didn't. Blake had been the guys' senior counselor last year, and he'd been involved in the whole process of her accusing Amber and Seth of sleeping together. Fortunately, he was greeting a couple of guys and busy with giving them instructions, so he didn't notice her presence until the girl beside him said her name.

"Hi, Elle. I'm Michaela. Let's see, I think you're my final counselor to arrive." She was looking at her list and put a check beside her name and then informed her which cabin was hers and handed her some papers and a bright red staff shirt.

Elle avoided Blake's eyes and felt very animated the entire time she was talking to Michaela and then as Nick checked in also and Michaela got him squared away. Nick was going to be on crew staff, but she had no doubt he would make friends quickly. She had told him it was okay for him to pretend he didn't know her, which he thought was ridiculous, but the thought of others treating him poorly because of her made her want to cry.

"Hi, Elle," Blake said, once the other guys had stepped away and she and Nick were about to do the same.

"Hi," she said. "How are you?"

"I'm good. How are you?"

"All right. This is my friend Nick."

Blake greeted Nick well, and Elle suddenly felt like she needed to address the issue instead of pretending it never happened. If seeing Blake was bringing her such a strong feeling of shame and the need to avoid a conversation with a completely respectable guy, she couldn't imagine how facing Amber and Seth would feel.

"Is Dave around?" she asked.

"Yeah, he's here. I'm not sure where. Do you want me to try and reach him on the radio for you?"

"Yeah, thanks. I'd really like to talk to him if possible."

***

"Yo, Warner!"

Warner turned to see one of his good friends jogging up the trail. He hadn't seen Adam since last summer, but he looked the same. It was good to see him.

"What are you doing up here?" Adam asked, referring to the crew housing area. "Aren't you counseling?"

"Not unless Blake needs me to," he said. "I requested crew team. It's more my thing."

Adam laughed. "I'm sure Seth will love having a strong guy like you around."

"Hopefully," he said. "I wouldn't mind counseling for high school, but little kids wear me out and junior-high boys get on my nerves."

Adam knew him well and didn't argue with him on that point. "Have you been assigned a job yet? We could get something together and catch up while we work."

"Yeah, sure," he said. "I just got here, so I'm taking my stuff in and then we can find something to do. Where's Lauren?"

"Getting unpacked."

"Are you two still together?" he asked as they stepped into the large cabin shared by all of the work crew guys.

"Yep. I'm not letting her go. How about you and Mariah? Is that still going on? I saw her here."

"Yes," he said, setting his things beside a bunk and tossing his sleeping bag on the bare mattress. "Can you believe it?"

"Almost a year, huh? That's a long time for you."

"I think she might be the one."

Adam didn't hide his shock. "*The one*. Really? Have you spent a lot of time with her since last summer?"

"Not face to face. I only saw her at Christmas and during Spring Break, but our other forms of communication have been all right."

"Is she counseling?"

"Yes. We'll have to be creative about finding time together this summer too."

***

Nick left the cafeteria to go find his room. He wasn't sure what Elle planned to do, but he knew she would be all right without any help from him. She was one of the strongest people he'd ever met, and he was so proud of her for doing this. He knew it wasn't easy for her to return here, but she had.

Following the path up to the staff housing area, Nick found the right cabin and stepped inside the large bunkhouse. Other guys greeted him, and he introduced himself. A year ago he wouldn't have been able to enter a strange place and meet new people, feeling this confident about himself and about being where he was supposed to be, but he'd been completely transformed during the last six months. Changed by Jesus, and he was never going back to his old self and his old life.

He had lived in a lot of confusion, anger, and despair for a long time, made really bad choices, hurt other people, and had no real reason to live. His high school years were spent going to school during the day, doing just well enough to pass his classes, and then getting drunk or stoned most nights whenever he could get away with it.

Mostly it had been an escape. It wasn't something he did to be cool with his friends. He didn't have any friends. It wasn't something he did to rebel against his mom and dad. They weren't around enough to notice. He felt unloved, worthless, and lost. Life was pointless. Meaningless. Empty. Why show up for reality when it was so bleak anyway?

That had changed when he met Elle. By some miracle he actually made it into college, and she'd been in his literature class at the University of Oregon during Winter Term. He liked to read, so it was his favorite class and the one he actually showed up for every time. Elle did too, and she was nice to him. They discovered they were both from Albany, but they'd gone to different high schools in the mid-sized Oregon town.

He thought she was beautiful, but he wasn't attracted to her in that way. He needed friendship more than he needed a girlfriend, but he looked forward to seeing her three days a week, and after a few weeks he felt like they were becoming friends.

One day after class he asked her if she wanted to get some coffee and talk about the book they had finished and were expected to write a ten-page essay on by the end of the next week. He'd liked the book because it made him think about a couple of different issues seriously, especially the meaning of life. Was it about accomplishing things, relationships, self-improvement, preservation, or something else? He'd related well to the main character and felt like most people would, but Elle had a different view of it, and that surprised him.

"He's just lost," she said.

"Lost?"

"He has no direction or purpose. He's searching, but he doesn't know what he's searching for. He says he wants love, but he doesn't know what real love is. He's searching for peace, but he's looking in all the wrong places. And frankly, I don't buy the ending. It's just another temporary fix like everything else that didn't work for him."

He was speechless. Had they read the same book? Was she living on the same planet as the rest of the human race? As far as he was concerned, this book had the answers he'd been looking for, and she was telling him it was a lie?

But there had been something about the way she spoke that made him want to hear more. If this wasn't the key to happiness, was there one? And did she have her own philosophy of what it was?

"So, what's *your* answer to the meaning of life?" he asked. "Is there one?"

"Yes, I think so," she said with a mixture of certainty and uncertainty.

"You don't sound too confident about that."

"I know what it is, I'm just not sure I have the courage to give in to it."

"What?"

"It's something he considered," she said, pointing to the book. "But he brushed it aside too quickly without looking at the whole truth, and I think I've done the same thing."

She'd gotten his full attention by that point. "What?" he repeated himself, feeling skeptical of her answer and on the edge of his seat to hear it.

"It's about God," she said. "Only not the vague god he explores, but the real God. The God who made us. The God the greatest piece of literature talks about. It's all there, we just have to be willing to take a good look at Him and believe it."

Elle's words had drawn him in, and he wanted to know more. She'd spent the rest of the day with him, and she explained the basics of the Bible and Christianity. She didn't claim to understand everything fully herself, and she freely admitted she'd failed in following some of its principles. But still, she was convinced God was the answer, and he'd been willing to explore the possibility that had changed his life.

And he knew the journey wasn't over yet. This was only the beginning.

Chapter Six

Seth was surprised by the number of older guys he had on crew staff. Normally it was made up of mostly high school students, and he'd been looking forward to taking on a mentoring role with them this summer. But several of the veteran staff members had requested to be on crew instead of counseling, and there were also a couple of new guys who were his age too.

He would have felt inadequate to be leading his peers, rather than guys who were younger than him, if it wasn't for the fact he'd been mentoring a lot of his peers all year at college. He'd deliberately not gotten involved in the youth program at church so he could have more time with Amber, but he ended up guiding a lot of guys through their first months of college—In their relationship with God, in their relationship with their girlfriend, and talking with them about the reasons behind the right choices they needed to be making.

He had the feeling this summer would be more of the same, and he didn't mind, but he had to shift gears in his mind by the time the afternoon was coming to an end and they were on their way to dinner. He shared that with Amber, but she had the opposite, mostly younger girls he had no doubt she would be a wonderful mentor to, and she seemed settled about keeping her focus on them this summer, not whatever happened with Elle. She amazed him. She always had, but especially in this. And not just now, but in the way she had handled the huge blow to her flawless reputation last summer.

They hadn't seen Elle yet today or heard if she'd arrived, but he fully expected to see her at dinner. He didn't have a plan for when that happened. Last night he'd been imagining different scenarios and how he would greet her, but it never seemed to be the same twice, and what Amber had said about letting Jesus carry them brought him the most peace. So he tried not the think about it and assumed he would make it through somehow. He felt more concerned for Amber than himself, but she didn't seem too concerned, so he tried not to be either. He could always deal with a major crisis moment when it came.

***

Mariah scanned the dining area for Warner, and she saw him talking to Adam. Crossing the room to say hi to Adam, whom she'd seen from a distance earlier but hadn't talked to, she gave him a hug and felt happy he was here again this summer. He was the type of guy she normally would have been attracted to last summer if it wouldn't have been for being more interested in his best friend. Without that tension of hoping he liked her, she'd been able to be more herself, and he had become a legitimate guy-friend, instead of one she pretended to be friends with just because she was hoping for something more.

She smiled at Warner also but didn't give him a hug. She had already given him one earlier after waiting for him to arrive, and giving him another one at this point would be more about their status as boyfriend and girlfriend than welcoming a friend she hadn't seen for awhile.

He did lessen the distance between them to whisper something in her ear—loud enough for Adam to hear but not anyone else who was close by. "He's surprised you've put up with me for this long."

"I didn't say that," Adam replied. "I said a year is a long time for you to be with the same girl."

"Same thing," he said.

Mariah smiled, but she didn't comment. She was more than surprised she'd managed to keep Warner's interest for this long. Last summer she had spent the first half of the summer having a major crush on him, even though he had another girlfriend. After they broke up, through absolutely no interference of her own, she'd been thrilled when he asked her to spend time with him on a Saturday a couple of weeks later, but to this day she wasn't certain why he had noticed her.

He was one of those guys who dated a lot of different girls, and usually the prettiest ones, but she had dated very little and didn't consider herself to be anything special beauty-wise. Just an ordinary girl with light red hair and freckled skin and basically no figure, but for some mysterious reason Warner had been interested, and nearly one year later he didn't seem at all anxious to go looking elsewhere.

Dave got their attention then, letting them know they could begin going through the food line. Mariah followed Adam and Warner to the counter between the dining area and the kitchen, but Warner let her go ahead of him in line.

Warner and Adam were talking casually with one another, and she mostly listened, but she didn't feel like Warner was ignoring her. Since seeing him earlier this afternoon, she knew she was getting clear signals he was happy they were here together. And even if they had been separated by distance for most of the last nine months, she felt they had developed a special connection that was real and deep, and exactly what she wanted out of a relationship.

Now the only question was, would it last?

***

Lauren entered the dining hall and saw Adam near the front of the line. She went to meet him and said hello to Warner and Mariah also. Glancing around the room, she checked to see if Elissa was here, and she wondered if Adam had seen her yet. She didn't think he knew she was going to be here, and she also didn't think Abby was too, but she wasn't certain.

Adam had dated both of them his first summer here, and neither relationship had been a positive experience for him. His relationship with Elissa had been short, and other than Elissa being emotional over the breakup, she didn't think it had affected Adam too seriously, so she wasn't that worried about it. But if Abby was here too, that could be a much bigger issue for him.

She didn't want to say anything right in front of Warner, but she didn't know if she should wait for him to discover it for himself. He could already know, and if Abby was here, he might have seen her, but she didn't think that could be the case with how easily he welcomed her and the relaxed mood he seemed to be in.

Since he was talking to Warner and they were next in line to get their plates, she decided to wait a few minutes and see if she had the opportunity to say anything. Turning her attention to the food being served, she felt her mouth watering at the sight of the brightly colored fruit salad with plenty of strawberries, and the baked potatoes followed by all the fixings. She loved camp food. Maybe too much. She had gained ten pounds last summer.

Once they had their food and were looking for a table, she scanned the room for either Elissa or Abby again but didn't see them. She followed Adam, who was following Mariah and Warner, and they sat at an unoccupied table. She saw Seth and Amber come into the room, and she wondered if they'd had any encounters with Elle yet. She hadn't seen Elle in the cabin area or anywhere around camp, but she'd heard from Blake she was here.

The one thing that kept her mind off all the potential drama of the evening was Warner. He was different. He'd always been on the cocky and arrogant side, and she hadn't liked him much—at least not as someone she would want to date. He was really good-looking, but Adam was much more her type. She'd been surprised when Warner started dating Mariah toward the end of the summer last year. Mariah was really sweet, but quiet, and she didn't have the look of girls Warner usually went for.

She hadn't seen them together enough last year to make a judgment about whether or not it would last. But seeing them together now, Lauren could see a serious relationship was forming between them. They lived about five hours from each other—Warner in Vancouver, Washington and Mariah in southern Oregon, so she knew they hadn't seen each other much during the last nine months, but that didn't seem to matter.

She became consumed enough with watching them she didn't notice when Elissa entered the room. Adam noticed before she did, and Warner noticed the ashen look on his face.

"What's wrong, man?" he asked.

Adam nodded Elissa's direction, and Warner turned to look. He didn't seem to recognize her at first, nor could he remember her name.

"Is that—?"

"Elissa," Adam said. Turning to her, he added, "Did you know she was here?"

"Yes, I saw her earlier, but I didn't talk to her."

"Who is it?" Mariah interrupted.

Warner laughed. "One of Adam's old girlfriends."

"Shut up, man," he said. "It was never official."

"Wasn't that a crazy summer?" Warner added. "Have you told Lauren about that?"

From the way Warner joked about it, Lauren doubted he knew the whole story about what had happened with Abby. Warner could be flippant about some things, but not when it came to his friend's good reputation.

"Yes," Adam simply said, glancing at her like he was more concerned about how she would react to Elissa and Abby being here than Warner's comments.

"Is Abby here too?" he asked her.

"I haven't seen her."

He sighed, and she laid her hand on his knee. Neither Warner nor Mariah commented on it further, and they didn't have to wait much longer before finding out the answer. Once Elissa had her food, she came to sit with them, not so much because she appeared to be looking for them specifically, but just because most of the other tables were full.

"Can I sit here?" she asked.

"Sure," Warner said. "Good to see you, Elissa. I didn't know you were going to be here."

"I am," she said. "How are you?"

"I'm good," Warner said. "This is my girlfriend, Mariah, and you know Adam, right?"

"Yes," she said. "And Lauren. I go to Lifegate too."

"Oh yeah?" Warner said. "Abby too?"

"Yes."

"Is she here?"

"No," Elissa said. "Just me."

That made Lauren feel better, and she supposed Adam did too, but she didn't have a chance to talk to him about it until later. Following dinner, Dave talked to them all about what they would be doing this evening, and then he dismissed them, but Lauren and Adam volunteered to help in the kitchen.

"You okay?" she asked once they were in the dish room and had a moment alone.

"Yeah," he said. "Elissa's okay without Abby. Are you okay?"

"Sure," she said.

He stepped closer to give her a hug and spoke serious words. "If she says anything to you about me and her or me and Abby, I want you to tell me, okay? No matter what it is."

"Okay. Same for you."

"I will, Angel."

"What's going on with Warner?" she asked, changing the subject.

Adam laughed and stepped away to start loading the dishwasher. "I'm not sure, but it sounds to me like he's finally falling in love."

***

Warner stepped outside with Mariah and asked what she wanted to do for the next hour before they had to be at the meeting scheduled for seven o'clock. He wanted time with her if possible. He hadn't had much today.

"Can we walk a little?" she asked.

"Sure."

She smiled at him, and he continued walking beside her up the path toward the lake. It was getting cool, and he offered to stop by his room and grab something warm for them so she wouldn't have to go back to her cabin. He hadn't unpacked at all, so he took two sweatshirts from his bag. His Portland State hoodie was huge on her, and she had to roll up the sleeves, but he thought she looked adorable.

Mariah wasn't a big talker, and they were both quiet for a few minutes as they headed back to the lake and began to walk the path surrounding it. He didn't mind her being quiet.

"Are you glad we're here together?" he asked.

"Yes. Are you?"

"I am."

She seemed satisfied with his answer and didn't do what a lot of girls did: asking him to back that up with all the "whys" and other relationship-talk that usually confused him. He liked girls. He liked being around them and was attracted to them easily, but most of the time he felt clueless about what they wanted.

He felt that way with Mariah too, but the difference was she seemed completely content to let him be who he was. He wasn't always sure she was happy, but she didn't complain or try to change him either. He never felt like she was judging him or expecting things from him he couldn't give.

"What was up with Adam at dinner tonight?" she asked. "He seemed a little disturbed about Elissa being here."

"I'm not sure," he said. "He dated her during our first summer, and it didn't end well. But they just went out a couple of times, and I think she read more into it than it was."

He thought back to that summer, trying to remember exactly what had happened. Adam had gone out with Abby too, but only once or twice. He'd never really known what had happened there, but he did remember his own experience with Abby.

He'd never been the type of guy to take advantage of a girl, even those he was highly attracted to, but if a girl was willing to give him a lot physically, he rarely tried to stop her. Abby was one he'd had to stop. Maybe Adam had encountered the same.

He also realized something else, now that he thought about his previous summers here and all the different girls he liked. Every summer, and during the school year back home, he was always on the lookout for his next girlfriend—sometimes before he'd broken up with his current one. It wasn't something he was proud of, and he knew it wasn't right to be thinking that way, but he really was searching for the right one and wanted to find her.

But today, being the first day of camp, and for the last nine months, he hadn't been looking. He was with Mariah, and he had no desire to look elsewhere.

"Am I doing that?" she asked, interrupting his thoughts.

"Doing what?"

"Reading more into this than it is?"

He recalled his comment about Elissa, and he understood why she would feel the need to ask. There was a lot more going on in his heart than he'd come out and said. He knew it was time to change that.

"I'm looking forward to having the summer with you," he said, stopping his stride and turning to look into her expressive green eyes. Right now they were speaking volumes about her insecurity mixed with a good dose of hope that something significant was happening between them.

He wanted to kiss her, but since he couldn't do that now, he knew he was going to have to say this. He couldn't keep her guessing all summer or even until next weekend when they would have more time together.

"If it wasn't for you, Mariah, I probably wouldn't be here."

She smiled. "I probably would be, but I'm glad you're here too."

"What brought you back besides me?"

"I just like it here. The people. The ministry. The spiritual emphasis. I need that."

"Yeah, me too," he said. "Last summer I kept thinking it would be my last year. Time to move on. Try something else. But I guess God had other ideas. He gave me the one thing it would take to bring me back."

"What's that?"

"You."

"And what am I?"

He was surprised at her boldness, but not that surprised. She often threw out things like that when he wasn't expecting it. He stepped forward and pulled her into a gentle hug, speaking the absolute truth.

"You're my best friend, Mariah, and I think I'm falling in love with you."

Chapter Seven

Amber and Seth met Dave on their way out of the dining hall, and he asked if he could speak with them privately in the office. They followed him to the small building across the deck and stepped inside. He asked them to close the door, and then he got straight to the point.

"I suppose you've noticed Elle's absence by now," he said.

"Yes," Seth replied for them. "Is she not coming?"

"No, she's here. She arrived this afternoon, but she's remaining in her cabin until something is settled."

"What?" Amber asked.

"She admitted to me today that she lied last summer, and I talked to her for a long time about why, which I'll leave up to her if she wants to share with you."

Amber knew she heard what Dave said, but she couldn't believe it. She'd been hoping for a lot of things this summer, mainly that she and Seth could go on with their lives in the midst of having Elle here, but she had never expected her to confess at this point.

"What does she want settled?" Seth asked.

"She wants to ask for your forgiveness."

Amber stared at Dave for a moment and then looked at Seth. Seth voiced what she was thinking.

"You're kidding."

"It looks like all those prayers you two prayed for her paid off. She's very sincere about this, and she's willing to leave if that's what you want."

Amber didn't know what to say, and Seth didn't seem to either. She finally spoke, feeling certain Seth would agree with her.

"I've already forgiven her, but if she wants to ask for that, I'm willing to let her."

"How did I know you were going to say that?" Dave said, stepping over to give her a hug. "You have a good heart, Amber, and Elle knows that. Last summer wasn't about you, it was about pain others caused her before she ever came here."

Dave left them in the office to go get other people, including Elle, and Seth took her into his arms and held her for a long time. She was in shock, but the reality began to sink in, and she realized how much she needed this. She'd been able to let go of everything except one part of her heart that sometimes wondered if Seth believed her. Seth had told her repeatedly he didn't believe Elle had seen her with someone else, but it felt good to have her name completely cleared.

"Thank you for always believing me, Seth."

"I did, sweetheart. I always did."

Before long, others joined them in the small office. Blake, who had been a part of this last summer, along with Michaela and Elle. Dave didn't waste any time and let Elle speak once they were all settled. Part of her expected Elle to be over-dramatic about it like she'd been last summer, but she wasn't that way at all. Dave's use of the word "sincere" fit perfectly.

"I'm sorry, Amber and Seth," she said. "I did a horrible thing to you. I lied, and I'm deeply sorry. I didn't come here to ask for your forgiveness, but once I was here I knew I had to. I know I don't deserve to be here, and if you want me to leave, I will."

"We don't want that, Elle," Seth answered for them. "We forgive you, and we want to put this in the past and move on with what we're all here for."

"Thank you," she whispered.

No one else said anything, and Dave led them all in a prayer. When he finished, he said they were free to go, and Elle rose from her chair. Amber met her in the middle of the room and initiated a hug.

Elle started crying at that point, and Amber held her until she stopped. The others slipped away quietly, except for Seth. After Amber released her, Seth stepped forward to give her a hug also, and Amber was reminded of what a loving heart he had. Not only for her and those close to him, but for anyone, even someone who had hurt him.

"I heard you got married," Elle said, wiping away her remaining tears and smiling. "Congratulations."

"Thank you," Amber said.

They let her go then, and once it was just the two of them, Seth did the same thing he had done before, holding her for a long time.

"Do you know what that was about, Amber?"

"What?"

"It was about your faith."

"What do you mean?" she asked, stepping back and looking into his serious face.

"Through all of this you've trusted Jesus to carry you. And in order to do that completely, He had to bring Elle to a point of repentance. Your faith, your unwavering trust in Jesus has resulted in her transformation."

"All I did was depend on Him for what I needed."

"Exactly!"

She smiled, understanding what Seth was getting at. "Not just me; you too. How many times did you tell me, 'Let's let Jesus be our defender.'?"

Amber walked around in a daze for the next couple of hours. She was interacting with others and engaging in the evening activities, but all the while she was thinking, 'I can't believe that happened. I can't believe all those prayers I whispered in anger and desperation and wishing good things for Elle resulted in that.' And yet she could. That was her God. And that's what He did.

***

Sienna hadn't planned to call Gabe for a few days, but by the time the clock said eight p.m., she felt like she had to. She'd been thinking the same thing all day, and if she tried to over-think this, she might talk herself out of it. It was a huge risk, but one she had to take.

Saying one last prayer before she did so, she called him, and when he picked up, she said she wanted to see him. He asked if tomorrow would be all right, and they agreed on a time. She wanted to meet him somewhere besides here and without Brittany for now.

"You can see her another time if you want, but I want you to be sure you want to first."

"Okay," he said. "And to be completely honest, I'm not sure I want to. Is that okay?"

"Yes. We can just talk, and whatever you want to say is what I want to hear, not what you think you should say."

"Can we talk for a little while now, or is this not a good time?"

"This is fine. Brittany is sleeping and won't need to eat for a couple of hours. Not that you have to talk for a couple of hours, just—this is fine."

"How are you?" he asked seriously.

"I'm okay. It's weird, having a baby and everything, but I'm okay."

"And how is she?"

"She's good. She's a good baby. Not too fussy or anything. It would probably be a lot harder if I was going to school or working right now, but I'm not, and my mom helps me a lot."

"That's good. How are you getting along with your mom and dad?"

"Okay. Some days are better than others."

"Do they know I called you?"

"No, not yet."

He didn't respond.

"Are you only doing this because of my dad?"

"No."

She wanted to ask him what he was thinking, but she decided to hold off on that for now. He talked about what he'd been doing since coming home from school and his summer job at Pizza Hut. He'd worked there during high school too, so she was familiar with some of the people he mentioned.

She asked him how his first year of college had been, and he said it had been okay. By twenty minutes into the call, Sienna could hear the lostness in Gabe's voice growing more and more, and that wasn't like him. He'd always been a confident person—a leader-type who knew what he wanted and went for it. But he didn't sound that way now.

She felt bad for the way she had seduced and lied to him, but she also wondered why he had given in to her in the first place. He could attract any girl just fine, and if he'd only been interested in sex from a girl, he probably could have gotten it from most. He hadn't needed her, and yet he spent a lot of time with her purely of his own free will—even when he had a perfectly good girlfriend waiting for him in Oregon.

She wanted to ask him if he'd talked to Rachael lately, but she decided to wait on that. She knew Rachael was with Josiah now, and she had heard rumors of their engagement.

When Gabe didn't attempt to end the conversation, she decided to let him go for now so they would have a few things to talk about tomorrow. He surprised her by saying something before telling her good-night.

"I think I'll be at church tomorrow. Are you going to be there?"

"Maybe," she said. "Sometimes if Brittany is up a lot in the night, I'm too tired to go."

"Well, if you are. I'll see you there."

It wasn't until after she hung up she realized he could be seeing Brittany tomorrow at church, and she wondered if he had considered that. Choosing to leave it in God's hands, she sat there and prayed for a long time. Not necessarily that Gabe would start loving her, but that she could follow the right paths Jesus had for her, whatever they were. She prayed the same thing for Gabe, something she hadn't done before.

She had a unique feeling in her heart. She wasn't sure what it was, but it was peaceful and it was good, so she clung to it.

***

Michaela couldn't believe how much fun she was having. It was only the first day of training week, and she already felt like she never wanted to leave this place or say good-bye to any of these people.

Her one stress of the day had been waiting to see what would happen with Elle, but meeting her initially had been fine, even pleasant, and being there to hear her confession and ask for Amber and Seth's forgiveness—she'd never seen anything like it. She'd heard about people making big turnarounds and people forgiving others who had hurt them, but she'd never been a part of it in a close-up way.

The first night was mostly about getting to know people, and Dave had several games, activities, and other creative ways of helping them accomplish that. She knew she would be getting to know certain people on a more individual level as the days progressed, but even in this crowd she felt close to everyone here already.

She tried to make a special point to connect with those who would be counseling, but she also had several random encounters. One was with a guy named Warner whom she thought was really cute, like most girls here would, but then she discovered he had a girlfriend, so she put her attraction for him aside immediately. The other was a guy named Nick who had an interesting quality to him she couldn't quite describe—a childlike wonder of this place and everyone here.

She learned later while they were having ice cream and hanging out that he was friends with Elle and that's how he'd ended up here. He didn't elaborate on that, but it made her curious. Were Nick and Elle together, or just friends? She certainly didn't want to get in the middle of something there, but at one point when the three of them were talking together, she didn't get a strong vibe there was any kind of attraction going on between them.

"Where did you disappear to earlier?" Nick asked Elle. "I thought maybe you dropped me off and then ran back home."

"I was in my cabin. I talked to Dave about wanting to confess my lie about Seth and Amber and ask for their forgiveness. And I didn't want them to have to face me until they knew that."

Nick smiled and gave her a hug. "That's great. I'm proud of you."

Michaela was standing there, but she didn't feel she was invading their privacy or listening in on a conversation that neither of them would want her to hear.

"Nick's my biggest fan," Elle said, wiping her tears away and giving her a smile that told Michaela he was special to her but in a brother-like way.

Training week was fun, a lot of hard work, and one of the best times Michaela could ever remember having. By Friday she had more new friends than she'd ever made in such a short time, and she had a few unique relationships she'd done little to bring about.

One of them was with Amber. Amber was everything she wanted to be, and she admired her so much. Amber wasn't older than her, and she didn't have any seniority over her in terms of their staff positions, but Michaela saw her as being someone she could learn a lot from and follow in many ways. Amber acted like she didn't know what she was doing, since she'd never been a senior counselor before either, but Michaela thought she was fantastic in everything she did.

She led the girls under her without being forceful or demanding. She handled difficult moments like they were nothing. She made serving God and others fun. She talked about Jesus like Michaela had never heard anybody talk about Him. And she always had time for anyone who needed something—even a listening ear.

Because they didn't have to be in all of the training meetings, and also because they had planning to do together for the staff girls, Michaela had several opportunities to talk with Amber purely on a personal level, and Michaela wasn't aware of a lot of the burdens on her heart until she was telling Amber about them.

She was stressed about her role here to some degree. She was clueless about her future and where she was headed. She was worried about some friends back home, from school, and family members. She was getting to know Nick better and was getting the impression he liked her, but she wasn't sure if she wanted to get into a relationship with someone here this summer, especially someone she wouldn't be able to see on a regular basis once the summer ended. And she had a lot of doubts about where her faith fit into the overall scheme of her life. She and Nick had talked about that a little, and he was looking for answers she should be able to give him, but she couldn't.

But no matter what the issue or problem, Amber's response was usually the same. 'Pray about it. I'll pray for you. Trust God. Give it to God. I used to feel that way, but then I learned to...'

She wanted to be like Amber, but she wasn't. But Amber made her feel like she could get there. One day at a time. One God-moment at a time. One faith-step at a time.

Chapter Eight

Gabe felt nervous about picking up Sienna at her house. Because their relationship had been a secret one, he'd never done so before, and even though her parents went to the church, he didn't really know them.

Their time together last Sunday had been okay. He'd been at church and seen her briefly there, but he hadn't sat by her or done anything to give anyone the impression they were together. It wasn't until he was there he realized he could also be seeing Brittany for the first time, and he didn't know if he was ready for that. Fortunately Sienna had already put Brittany in the nursery by the time he arrived, and then he left right after the service.

Seeing her later in the afternoon in a more private setting had been mostly good. She looked well, and she was different. More content. More at peace with her life and those in it. Cautious with him and yet open at the same time.

He had called her a couple of times this week, and on Thursday they had agreed to see each other again. But she hadn't wanted to meet him somewhere. She wanted him to face her mom and dad, see Brittany, and take her out like it was a date. She didn't expect him to say things he didn't mean or act in ways he wasn't ready for, but she wanted this to be something they didn't need to hide if he was sincere about it.

He wasn't sure he wanted this to go beyond having a healthy closure to their relationship, but he did feel he was sincere in wanting to have time with her, no matter what the results ended up being. Ringing the doorbell and stepping back to wait for the door to open, he felt most nervous about seeing her dad again. Mr. Johnson had been very mad and direct when he spoke to him before, and Gabe knew he couldn't give him the words he wanted to hear now either. He wasn't doing this to 'Be a man and take responsibility for his actions.' He wasn't sure why he was doing it and didn't feel prepared to answer that question.

But Sienna opened the door and welcomed him inside. She didn't appear nervous and didn't turn this into some grand thing it wasn't. Leading him into the kitchen where her mom and dad were getting ready to sit down to dinner, she simply introduced his presence, allowed them to have a cordial exchange, and then led him down the hall.

"She's sleeping," she said when they reached the right door. "I tried to keep her awake, but she was tired, and I didn't want to leave her fussy for my mom."

"Okay," he said, knowing this was a big deal and yet feeling indifferent to it.

Sienna stepped into the dimly lit room, and he followed her. The crib was along one wall, and they both stepped over to it. Brittany was lying on her back, sound asleep, with a light blanket covering her legs and torso.

As soon as his eyes fell on her, Gabe couldn't look away. He'd never seen a baby that was just sleeping like that so close up before. She was beautiful and looked peaceful. A unique feeling entered his heart.

He kept staring at her and allowed a reality to enter his mind. *That's my daughter.* It wasn't a scary thought or a threatening one, just a reality he could no longer ignore, and he was surprised he didn't want to. He knew Sienna was looking at him, and he swallowed hard, feeling like he should say something but unable to form the words.

He felt Sienna take his hand, and he kept looking at Brittany.

"We can go now," she said. "I just wanted you to see her."

Two minutes ago he had been anxious to get out of this house, but now he didn't want to leave.

"Okay," he said, turning his eyes from Brittany and looking at Sienna for the first time since they'd entered the room. He saw her differently too. Last Sunday he'd been thinking of her as the casual friend she had once been, but right now their intimate times came to mind, and his heart stirred at the thought of being with her.

She let go of his hand, and they went out. Other than stopping by her room to get her purse, their exit from the house wasn't delayed, and soon enough they were in the car and on their way to what he'd intended this night to be: spending time with Sienna and seeing if he could love her. But his mind wasn't focused on that anymore.

Something he couldn't explain had entered his heart. Maybe it was the shock of seeing Brittany for the first time and not expecting that to affect him so strongly, but when he was still thinking about it after dinner and while they were sitting in the theater waiting for the movie to begin, he began to accept another possibility.

Turning to Sienna, he knew he'd been quiet for the past hour, and he knew he had to say this or he might never say it. He could go on with his life and never admit seeing Brittany had any effect on him whatsoever, but he had a feeling he would be miserable if he did, and he would never be able to completely shake it.

He might go on to marry someone else, have other children, and live a good life, but that image of Brittany lying in her crib so peacefully would always remain, and the possibility of what might have been would haunt him. Even now he could feel it, and he couldn't let it go.

He started to speak, but Sienna spoke first. "Gabe, if you don't want to do this, just say so. We can go, and you can take me home, and you never have to see me again. I'll be all right. If you don't want this, I don't either."

Her words were sincere and had an air of peace to them he knew was completely genuine. And he didn't feel like he had to take care of her and Brittany. He was certain a noble guy out there would do a much better job, and if Sienna was meant to marry someone else who would love her with all of his heart, he would wish that for her in a heartbeat. He wanted her to be happy, not stuck in a marriage her guilt-ridden husband didn't want.

"I don't think I can sit through a movie right now," he said. "Can we go?"

"Yeah, sure," she said.

He could see the disappointment in her eyes, but she wasn't going to argue with him. He would have told her the real truth about why he didn't think he could sit through a movie right now, but the previews were starting, and he knew it would be better to continue this conversation outside.

***

Sienna felt determined to not cry. She was disappointed Gabe didn't want to be a part of Brittany's life, but she didn't blame him either. She knew it had to be very overwhelming for him. She had seen it in his eyes when he'd been looking at Brittany earlier.

He'd gone almost completely silent on her after that, appearing shell-shocked but also thoughtful, and she had allowed herself to hope he might consider giving this a try, but when he looked at her in the theater just now, she'd known what he was going to say, so she said it for him.

Waiting for Gabe to open the car door, she wouldn't have looked at him or said a word, except he didn't make any move to unlock the door. When he just stood there, she looked up at him, and she could tell he had something to say.

"I'm okay, Gabe, really." She wasn't lying. She had prepared herself for this possibility from the beginning and knew she would be okay eventually. She was disappointed, but she still had hope God had someone else for her, and she would cling to that.

"I wasn't going to say I don't want this, Sienna," Gabe said with a shaky voice. "I was going to say I can't sit through a movie right now b-because I'd rather go back to the house and see Brittany again."

Her heart warmed at his tone. It reminded her of the way he had sometimes spoken to her before their relationship became a physical one—back when they were friends and he would open up to her and share things on his mind and heart. Honest things. Personal things. Things he had never told anyone else. Things that made her feel a special connection to him. She'd almost forgotten that.

"Why do you want to see her?" she asked.

"I can't get her out of my mind. I didn't want to leave the room. That's my—"

He didn't finish, but Sienna knew he was being honest with himself and her, and she knew she had to grant his request. She wanted to. How many times had she prayed for this exact thing?

"We can go," she said. "She is yours, Gabe, and you can have as much time with her as you want."

"I can't promise you anything right now, Sienna, but I know I need to do this. Is that okay?"

"Yes."

Gabe drove to the house, and neither of them said anything. Leading them to the front door and inside the foyer, Sienna thought Brittany might still be sleeping, but she heard cries coming from the living room. Rounding the corner, she saw her mom trying to give her a bottle, but she didn't seem to want it.

She took Brittany from her mother's arms and lifted her onto her shoulder. Her mother explained she woke up fifteen minutes ago and was fussy, but she hadn't eaten much.

"I don't think she can be hungry yet," she said, looking at the clock. "Must be something else."

Gabe had remained in the doorway of the living room, and rather than inviting him to come join them, she decided to take Brittany to her room and give them space to be alone. She knew Gabe would be more comfortable there than under the watchful eyes of her parents. Her dad wasn't in the room currently, but that could change quickly. She appreciated her dad's concern and effort to talk to Gabe, but she felt bad for the way he'd chosen to go about it. Gabe might not be completely innocent in all of this, but he hadn't deserved that.

Once they were in Brittany's room, she told him to close the door, and she patted Brittany until she began to relax in her arms. She wasn't completely content, but her loud crying had stopped, and Sienna knew she was either just tired or had a tummy ache.

Looking at Gabe, she saw his eyes were on Brittany, and she continued to hold her until she heard her burp a little. Once Brittany was completely calm, she asked Gabe if he wanted to hold her.

He didn't answer.

"Come here," she said. "Sit in the chair, and I'll hand her to you."

He obeyed but looked petrified. She stepped over and lowered Brittany into his arms. He held her awkwardly at first, but she told him to relax his arms and lean back in the rocker. He did and Brittany wasn't too disturbed by the transition. Sienna reached for her pacifier and gave it to her, and she seemed content with the temporary comfort measure.

Gabe couldn't take his eyes off her, and Sienna let him stare in wonder. She'd been the same way right after Brittany had been born and for several days afterwards. She remembered thinking, 'Where did you come from, and why are you here with me?'

Gabe held her for a long time, and Brittany eventually closed her eyes and went to sleep. When Gabe finally looked up, he had tears glistening in his eyes. Sienna felt amazed this was happening, but it was exactly what she had prayed for—not so much with words, but with her heart.

Chapter Nine

"Why do we have to practice getting married?" Kevin asked for the billionth time.

Kerri laughed and leaned back into her fiancé's arms. "You know why," she said.

"No, I don't," he teased innocently. "Why?"

She turned around and gave him the same answer she'd been giving him all day. "So we can practice kissing and get it just right."

"Oh, yeah," he said, giving her a sweet kiss in the middle of the chaotic rehearsal. "I forgot."

"We're almost done," she said, saying the words for herself as much as him. This was taking longer than she wanted it to. Currently her sister was practicing her solo, but they were having trouble with the sound system.

Pastor John came over to discuss what they wanted to happen after Erika sang, and Kerri didn't care at this point. "What do we have left?"

"The unity candle, communion, and the prayer."

"How about if we do the unity candle while Erika is singing, and then you can pray, and we'll skip communion."

"Whatever you want," he said. "I get paid either way."

"And we get married either way," she laughed.

"All right then," he said, making some notes and taking charge of the moment. "Erika, let's have you practice tomorrow after they figure out what's wrong back there. I'm going to pray now, and then we'll be done."

Pastor John prayed seriously for them and the wedding tomorrow, and then he raced over the last part where he pronounced them man and wife, they kissed, and the music began and they descended the stage. But Kevin protested.

"We have to practice the kiss," he said. "Right, Kerri?"

She smiled. "Yes. We should practice that."

Kevin never held back when he kissed her, even if others were around, and she allowed him to set the pace for this "practice" kiss.

Several people were laughing by the time he finished, but neither of them cared. "How was that?" Kevin asked.

"Perfect," she said.

They walked together down the aisle then, and once they were outside the auditorium, Kevin kissed her again, and she felt so ready to marry him for real.

"Hey, what's going on here?" she heard someone say. Turning to look across the expansive lobby, she saw Seth and Amber coming toward them, and she smiled.

Kevin released her, and she stepped over to give her brother a hug. She hadn't seen him for almost two weeks, and their last time together had been brief, just a couple of hours on the night she had returned from California. Amber and Seth had left for camp the next day.

Seth held her for a long time, and she was glad she'd asked him to come tonight instead of not being able to see him until tomorrow when everything was more hectic. She had told them they didn't need to come for the rehearsal since neither of them were in the wedding, but she'd asked if they could come for the dinner they were planning afterwards.

"It's going to be great, Kerri," he said. "The wedding, the honeymoon, your marriage, everything."

"Speaking from experience on that?"

"Absolutely."

They all went to dinner then, and it was a good time. A time to relax with her family and friends. A time to be with Kevin one last time before they moved into a new stage of their relationship. And a time to be reminded of all that had led her here. All the prayers. All the difficult but good choices. All the mistakes she'd learned from. And all the moments she'd had with Kevin during the last ten months—from meeting him at Tony's and helping him make pizza, to going to his recital and not running from the surprising outcome, to allowing herself to fall in love with him without having to know all the details of how their relationship was going to work. She'd gone with her heart, and that had led her to this: something she'd always dreamed of but had seemed very scary at times.

Kevin had been staying at her house since arriving last weekend, but with his family in town tonight, he was planning to stay with them at the hotel.

"If you need to call me tomorrow or come by the house, you can," she said. "Whatever you need, I want you to do that, all right?"

"Okay," he said.

"I love you, Kevin. I can't wait to spend the rest of my life with you."

He kissed her, and she cherished his touch. His sweet lips that were only for her and his gentle hands that never touched her inappropriately. That would be changing tomorrow, only it wouldn't be something that would damage her spirit; it would be something loving, and something she could give to Kevin, rather than have him take it from her.

"Will you be at the church tomorrow?" he asked. "Promise?"

"Yes, I promise. I'll be there."

***

Before heading for their cabins, Mariah and Warner decided to find a quiet place to sit during the remaining half-hour they had before lights-out. She'd had a bit of a difficult week because she got sick on Tuesday, waking up with a bad sore throat and cough that kept her in bed for two days. She had terrible body aches and a headache one day, but she was feeling better today and had been able to participate in the evening activities.

Warner had been sweet through it all, bringing her soup several times and sitting with her while she rested in the health center whenever he had the chance. She knew she'd been sleeping some of the time and had missed him, but the camp nurse always let her know he'd been there.

His attentiveness surprised her. Last year they had only gone out on a couple of Saturdays before the end of the summer, and during the week their time together had been limited. She hadn't really counted on it lasting beyond the summer, and Warner hadn't given her a lot of reason to hope for it, so she hadn't. He asked for her phone number, but she'd been surprised when he called, and furthermore when he kept calling, usually twice a week.

She began writing him letters, and he kept calling, and that had been the totality of their relationship. He'd only kissed her a couple of times. Once on their second date together, and once on the staff retreat the following weekend. And neither kiss had been especially good. Not horrible, but not something that said, 'I really like you' either.

That changed when she saw him during Winter Break. He'd driven down to Ashland to spend two days with her, and at first it had been a lot like the end of the summer, only they had gotten to know each other better by then.

But when he kissed her that first night while they went for a walk around her neighborhood, it had a different quality to it. One that matched his willingness to drive five hours to see her. One that matched his frequent phone calls and the way he could talk to her for an hour. One that made her feel like something real was happening between them.

Her time with him during Spring Break had been similar, and when they both decided to spend the summer here again, she had every reason to believe they would be spending more time together, and yet his constant attention this week had taken her by surprise. He knew other people here, and there were plenty of new friends for him to make, but his primary focus was her—even when he could have easily left her alone these last few days.

Walking beside her to the deck off the dining hall where they could sit, Warner asked if she had any plans for tomorrow. Several of their friends were going to Portland for Kerri's wedding, but she hadn't gotten to know Kerri all that well and didn't have a strong desire to go, especially since she wasn't feeling super-great.

"Whatever you're doing," she said.

He smiled. "Even if that's taking you to the beach?"

"You don't want to go to the wedding?"

"Not especially," he said. "Unless you want to."

She asked him something she had often wondered. "Did you ever date Kerri?"

He laughed. "No. She wouldn't give me the time of day."

"But you were friends."

"Friends, yes. Kerri is willing to be friends with anybody. But as a boyfriend, she had specific criteria she was looking for, and I didn't come close."

Mariah remembered thinking that about Warner herself. After admiring him from a distance most of the summer, she discovered some things about him that were questionable when they'd actually gone out. Nothing major like him being disrespectful of her or trying to go too far physically, but he could be a little arrogant at times and seemed to not take his relationship with God too seriously. He'd been a counselor last summer, but he didn't have a lot of patience with kids, and he talked about other people behind their back.

But over the course of the year while they'd been in contact with each other on a weekly basis, she sensed him changing. He talked about God more and more, others less and less, and he seemed more concerned for those he normally would have brushed aside as being flaky and not worth his time. It had been difficult to know if he was talking differently or if he'd changed, but this week she had seen enough to know his actions were matching his words. He had a good heart, he'd just needed to grow into it more.

"I'd love to go to the beach," she said. "As long as you don't mind a relaxing day. I'm not up for anything too active."

"I'll take care of you," he said. "We can't have one of the best counselors here all tired-out the first week."

"You're glad you're not counseling, aren't you?"

"Yes," he said. "It's way more work than anything I'll ever do on crew."

"You'd better pray no one gets sick, or you'll be the first one in."

"Oh? Have you been kissing any other guys who will be catching what you had?"

"No, I haven't even kissed you."

"Not yet."

She was looking forward to being kissed by him tomorrow, but she had something she wanted to ask him. They'd been communicating with each other all year, but she hadn't seen it as them having an exclusive relationship. She hadn't dated anyone else, and he hadn't mentioned other girls, but she didn't know for certain he hadn't been dating here and there.

"Have you kissed anyone besides me since last summer?"

Whether he said yes or no she didn't care, and she expected him to laugh when he gave his answer either way, but he didn't. Reaching over and gently taking her hand from her lap, he answered seriously.

"No, Mariah. I haven't. Just you."

She smiled. The few kisses they'd shared became more special to her. More special for them.

"Have you kissed anyone else?" he asked.

"No."

"Your friendship has changed me, Mariah. Do you realize that?"

"I like you better this way. I think this is the real you."

"I hope so. I like me better this way too. I like me better with you."

Mariah knew that was a good note to end on, so she told him she felt tired and said good night. Once she was out of his line of sight, she sighed and couldn't believe this was happening. She'd never felt this way, and she didn't know how to describe it. Finding love with Warner hadn't come easily, but it had come, and she was almost afraid to hope for anything beyond this, but she couldn't help it. She didn't want this feeling to go away. She didn't want Warner to stop letting her into his heart.

Loving him made her feel alive. And being loved by him made her love him even more. She knew it was dangerous. She knew Warner could break her heart into a million pieces, but guarding her heart wasn't an option. Not taking the chance would be worse than Warner disappointing her in the end.

She had been keeping a diary of their relationship, from the day he asked her out until the present. Some days she had a lot to write, others nothing, but she'd been writing a ton this week, especially last night when she rested instead of participating in the evening activities but was feeling well enough to sit up and write about the previous two days.

Once she got into bed, she left the light on above her bunk, and she wrote about Warner asking her to go to the beach tomorrow, and then she wrote exactly how she was feeling.

I really do love him, Jesus. I want good things for him. I want him to believe he can love someone genuinely and be at peace in that love. His heart is so beautiful to me right now, and I don't want him to let go of that.

All along I've told you I have no idea what I'm doing in this relationship. And all along you've kept telling me, 'Just be you, Mariah. Just rest in My love and let Me take care of Warner. You don't have to change him, I will. Just be his friend, that's all he needs from you.'

I didn't always believe you, but what he said tonight was like an exclamation point on all of that. Thank you for giving me the strength to keep going with this even when I was afraid of him not returning that friendship and ending up with an empty heart. You kept filling it, and now

Warner is too. I know you won't stop, and I pray he won't either.

Chapter Ten

The only wedding Chad could remember being at in all of his growing-up years was when he was eight and his mom had married his stepdad. At the time he didn't understand what marriage was. His dad had left when he was very young, and once his stepfather moved into the house and knocked him and his mom around a few times, Chad didn't have a good view of marriage from that point on.

He'd learned to see it as something that worked for people like Seth's parents, but not everyone. And even though his mom and stepdad had remained together for more than ten years now, he had often wished they would get divorced. They had times where they seemed to do all right, but then something would erupt and the effects would last for weeks or months. There had been a couple of times when his stepfather had left and been gone for several days, and he always hoped he wouldn't come back.

Since he'd been away at school this year, he had asked his mom regularly if "Dad" was treating her and his younger siblings all right, and his mom always said he was. He hoped she wasn't lying. He prayed for his family every night, and he'd been trying to believe God would bring peace to their home.

After not attending any weddings for a long time and having a mostly negative view of marriage, he'd been to two weddings in the span of three weeks' time, and there would be a couple more before the summer was over. Three weeks ago he'd watched his best friend marry the love of his life, and today it would be Seth's sister Kerri doing the same. They were both very special people to him, and he couldn't be more happy and supportive of their decisions, and yet there was an unsettled feeling in his heart about whether or not he would ever be able to do the same.

He wanted to believe he could be a good husband to Jessica and they could have the best kind of marriage, but could they? Really? With the examples he'd been raised with? What did he know about making a marriage work? How did he know he wouldn't resort to anger when things didn't go his way or they were facing financial hardship? How did he know he would never let Jessie down? What did he know about loving a woman for the rest of his life?

Some days he felt like he wanted to marry Jessica tomorrow, and then other times he felt certain it would never happen. He would rather let her go than make a commitment to her he wasn't certain he could keep.

"Oh, isn't it beautiful?" Jessica said, taking his arm as they stepped into the sanctuary of the church. Kerri had chosen white flowers, and they were everywhere, including two large displays on the stage along with a white arbor that was covered with so much foliage it was a wonder the thing didn't tip over.

"It's nice," he said, not expecting anything less from Kerri and the family she came from. He could imagine Jessie choosing something similar, but would he be the one she would want to take as her husband when it came down to it?

They were seated near the front, and they were a little early, so he had a lot of time to dwell on his conflicting thoughts and emotions. After a few minutes, Jessica took his hand and said something she'd never talked about before.

"I've always wanted to get married in my backyard with just a few guests," she said. "It's beautiful but not as large as Amber's, so we'd have to keep the guest-list small. What do you think of that?"

He looked at her, and he didn't know what to say. He hadn't missed her use of the word "we" in her statement. They'd talked about getting married following Seth and Amber's wedding, but neither of them had mentioned it since. Not until now.

"I like your backyard," he said.

She didn't comment further, and he didn't get the impression she was looking for him to elaborate on that, so he let it be. He didn't see her question as being a manipulative one, she was just sharing her thoughts freely with him like she always did, but it remained on his mind as they waited for the ceremony to begin.

Chad had gotten to know Kevin pretty well after working with him at Tony's, and he'd seen Kerri and Kevin together enough to know they were a good match and very much in love. He didn't question Kevin's ability to love Kerri; If there was one thing Kevin knew how to do better than anyone, it was to love people. And it wasn't something he did as much as a natural expression of his personality. Kevin didn't just know how to love, he didn't know how to not love.

But Kevin had a special love for Kerri that was plain to see. And while he'd been a little shocked at Kerri's decision to marry him this soon, he wasn't surprised. Kevin was a difficult person to put on hold for anything, especially someone he was so passionate about. Kerri wasn't just in his life, she had become his life, and Chad couldn't be happier for both of them.

The ceremony had a romantic feel to it without being too much. It was simple but rich in love and sacredness that felt tangible to him. He'd been holding Jessie's hand, but when Kerri's sister sang a beautiful song, he had to pull her closer to him. She smelled good today, even more than usual, and she had her hair done in a beautiful way, and her dress was elegant and soft.

Closing his eyes, he could imagine her wearing a bridal gown and them standing together up on that stage, or in her backyard. He didn't think it would matter to him where they were because all he would see was her.

***

After lighting the unity candle with Kevin, Kerri stepped back to their spot in front of the arbor that smelled of fragrant, fresh flowers, and she took Kevin's hands and just looked at him as her sister hit the chorus of the song. It was a song she had never heard until Kevin had played it for her a few weeks ago. But as soon as she heard it, she agreed with him it would be perfect for their wedding. The chorus was simple but so true, an expression of the way she felt about her love for Kevin and his love for her.

I love you loving me
And I need it every day
Without your love, life would go on
But I'm not sure about me

And when I'm loving you
My heart feels so complete
Like an ever-flowing fountain
When I'm loving you

She smiled at Kevin, feeling amazed by how well he was doing today. He didn't look nervous at all, and that wasn't something he could hide, so she knew he really wasn't.

We're getting married, baby. Just like you wanted. And I couldn't be happier.

She couldn't tell him that right now. They'd already spoken standard vows, and following this song they would only be a few heartbeats away from being pronounced husband and wife, but she felt connected to Kevin on such a heart level it was all just a formality. Man's way of joining two lives together. But God was doing the real work here, and He'd started a long time ago when He led her to California to meet Kevin at a place where a friend of hers worked who she'd met on another God-seeking path.

When Kevin kissed her today, it felt the same as always, and yet a little different. She knew he didn't understand all the changes between them that marriage would bring, and she didn't know a lot of them either—at least not from a firsthand point of view, but Kevin didn't need to know. All he knew was he loved her, and he was happy when he loved her. In his mind their love could never end. That possibility would never enter his thought process. Love was a never-ending thing, and this was just another stage of the journey.

They had a simple reception in the fellowship hall downstairs. She hadn't wanted to overwhelm Kevin with too many wedding festivities, so cake and finger-foods were served inside while they stood on the back patio and allowed their guests to come to them and offer their congratulations and well-wishes.

When she got to the point where she was feeling overwhelmed with the day, she knew Kevin likely was too, and she asked him if he wanted to go. They hadn't set an exact time for leaving, but she hadn't figured on staying much later than this.

"Yeah," he said. "I feel tired."

"Me too. Let's go to the beach."

He pulled her close and kissed her. "I can sleep with you tonight," he said like he was informing her of the news.

"I know," she said, kissing him in return. "And I can't wait."

***

Mariah didn't know what to expect from Warner today. When they'd gone to the beach together last summer, they hadn't known each other very well and did standard tourist things in Newport. She remembered having the feeling Warner had done the same with a lot of other girls, and their day had been more about activity than being there together. He could have been with someone else and had the same experience.

It had been different when he'd come to see her during Winter Break and then again in the spring, because she had been the one to lead him around an unfamiliar town, and if they weren't out doing something, they were at her house. They spent a lot of time talking and getting to know each other, but they were in that stage of neither of them having any sense of what their time together was really about or where they might be headed.

In her mind she pictured a similar day with him today, but in her heart she was hoping for much more. The short amount of time they'd had together this week had been of a different quality than before, and she wanted more of that. More of Warner's heart he'd been slowly opening to her. And more of an opportunity to give him her heart in return. She always gave him everything she could, but giving him love was limited by his readiness to accept it.

They stopped for lunch on the way and didn't arrive in Newport until one-thirty. Warner was a Marine Biology major, so he took her to some tide-pools he had visited with his classmates this spring. She remembered him telling her about it during one of their phone conversations, and she could tell it was something that really interested him.

She wasn't a big science person, but she enjoyed seeing all the different creatures living in the unique ecosystem. There were sea lions swimming around in one of the large pools, and they were able to get pretty close to them with Warner leading her silently across the exposed rocks.

It was a nice day for the Oregon Coast, but the cool air and wind made her start coughing, and he didn't let them stay too long after that. She said she felt better than she sounded, but he took her to get clam chowder where they could sit for a long time and watch people flying kites and building sandcastles on the beach from the restaurant window. He talked about his future career dreams, more so than he had before, and she hoped they came true for him.

She wasn't as certain about what she wanted to do. Things that interested her like nursing or caring for animals, she didn't feel like she had the science aptitude for, and her strengths like writing, literature, and history, she didn't know what to do with. She knew she would like teaching, but she wasn't sure she had the personality and presence to handle a room-full of kids. She was also thinking about going to cooking school but wasn't sure she could handle the stress.

He listened to her thoughts on all of that, and his response in the end surprised her. "You're a lot stronger than you think, Mariah. Whatever you end up choosing, I'm sure you'll be great at it."

"What makes you think so?" she asked, wanting to hear more on that if he was willing to share. He rarely commented on anything related to her personality or what exactly he liked about her. What he'd said this week about her friendship being so valuable to him had been the first time he ever talked about their relationship in those terms.

"You have qualities I can't begin to touch, Mariah. Inner qualities most of us have to work on, but they're just a part of who you are. So much so, you don't even realize it."

She wasn't sure what to say. "Like what?" she asked when she couldn't think of a single one.

"Your kindness," he said easily. "Your quiet strength that doesn't force other people to notice you but draws them in eventually—even tough cases like me. Your loyalty: Other than Adam being my best friend at camp for the last three summers, you're the longest-lasting close friend I've ever had. Your courage to do things that are scary, like counseling for a whole summer, and dating me," he laughed. "Need I go on?"

She mirrored his warm smile and almost said, 'Please do,' but she could be satisfied with those for now. He added one more.

"You're secure in who you are. Most girls aren't, even those who pretend to be. And I know I've never been that way."

Feeling bold and honestly wanting to know the answer, she asked him something point-blank. "Why are you with me? Because I'm a good person you admire, or is there more to it?"

He smiled. "How about if we discuss that on the walk I promised you? That's a good question, and I know the answer if you want to hear it."

Chapter Eleven

Walking on the moist sand along the water's edge, Mariah waited for Warner to speak. He was holding her close to his side with his arm around her waist, and it was the first time he'd ever walked with her that way. He usually held her hand and occasionally put his arm around her shoulder, but this said something different to her. This said, 'I don't just want to be with you, I want to be close to you.' And she hoped that was an inward reality of his heart too.

"So, why am I with you? Is that what you asked me?" he said.

"Yes."

He laughed. "For a long time I asked myself the same question."

She didn't respond and waited for him to go on. He began by explaining why he asked her out initially. Last year he had a girlfriend when the summer began, someone from his church back home he'd talked into spending the summer at camp, but they had decided after six weeks to just be friends—a common thing for him. He said it had ended well and they were still friends.

"Sometimes the reason I've broken up with girls is because I've become interested in someone else, but that wasn't the case with Heather. We had a lot of fun together, but otherwise we were both looking for something else.

"After we broke up, I felt a little lost, and I hadn't been looking elsewhere, so I spent a couple of weekends just hanging out with the gang, but I've always been better in one-on-one situations. That's why I've dated a lot. I feel like I get to know girls better that way.

"I began to feel like I needed to go out with someone, but I wasn't sure who to ask. A couple of the girls I thought I would like hanging out with were either dating someone or I didn't have the chance to talk to before Saturday."

Mariah knew what Warner was going to say next, but she let him say it.

"And then on Friday you brought your group up to Hidden Falls while I was there with my guys, and I saw you differently, I guess. I didn't really know you, but I knew you were a nice girl I'd probably enjoy spending the day with, so I asked."

"You were desperate," she laughed.

"No," he said. "I've never asked a girl out because I was desperate. There has to be something there, and there was. I was curious about you."

He stopped walking and stepped in front of her, blocking the mild wind. He kept his hand on her lower back and lifted his other fingers to her cheek. Looking into her eyes with absolute sincerity, he spoke his next words like he was amazed by the course their relationship had taken since then.

"I was curious, and after one date I was left wanting more of you. I know it's been a slow road, Mariah, but it's led me someplace I wasn't sure I'd ever find with anyone."

"Where?" she whispered.

He kissed her softly. "Being in love with you."

He kissed her again, in a different way than he ever had before. More personal and intimate without being too much.

"That's why I'm with you," he said. "You're my dream-girl, the one I've been searching for, and I never want to let go."

He kissed her for a long time, and it was soft and tender and amazing. A gentle passion she got the impression he had never experienced before. Like it wasn't even about their lips touching, but their souls.

"I don't want to go back," he said, holding her fully in his arms and taking a deep breath. "I don't want to be away from you for the next six days."

"I think we'd better," she laughed. "Six days of this would—"

"Six minutes, Mariah. So don't let me get away with anything, okay?"

She took his words seriously. "Okay."

He held her for another few moments but then released her and began walking again. She had been asking him bold questions today, and she had one more she felt it was the appropriate time for.

"Are you a virgin, Warner?"

"Yes. Are you?"

"Yes."

Warner wasn't surprised by Mariah's response, but he was a little surprised when she didn't say something about being surprised he was. Even when they'd been together this week, several people who knew him well had made teasing comments about what a nice girl like her was doing with him. She'd always been sweet about it, never questioning his reputation or past experience with dating that others often saw as flippant and fickle.

He knew some people saw him as the kind of guy who dated a girl long enough to get what he wanted from her physically and then moved on to the next, but it wasn't true. He'd struggled with his physical desires at times, especially with certain girls, but he'd also broken up with them for that reason—especially if they were the ones who were always tempting him.

Realizing he'd never asked her the question others had this week, he supposed this was the perfect time. "And why exactly are you with me, Mariah? Not just now, but all this time?"

"God told me to stick with it, so I did."

He laughed. "That sounds like you've had a really bad year."

"No, not bad," she said, giving him a sweet smile. "Just a little confusing. I didn't think you liked me, but you kept calling."

"I did like you. I liked talking to you. But I wasn't sure if I had more to give you than friendship, so I didn't want to give you that impression."

She was silent for several moments, but he had the feeling she had something to say. He squeezed her hand and pulled her closer to his side. "I'm sure now," he said to make that clear to her. "I want you to believe that, okay?"

"Okay," she said, but there was reservation in her voice.

He wondered if he had said too much. Was she not ready to be in love? Had she been happy with the way things were between them and now he was giving her more than she wanted?

He started to feel a familiar discomfort. Reading girls had never been his strength. He needed them to tell him what they were thinking and what they wanted. At this point he would give Mariah whatever she needed from him, but he couldn't if he didn't know what that was.

He stopped walking, knowing he couldn't handle any miscommunication between them right now. He had opened his heart to her fully, but he felt insecure about it. He was falling in love with her and wouldn't blame her if she wasn't sure she could go there with him, but he didn't want her faking anything.

"Did I say too much?" he asked.

She looked up at him in surprise. "No."

"Is that what you wanted to hear?"

"If it's true."

He smiled. "It is. I wouldn't say it if it wasn't."

"I'm glad," she said. "I'm falling in love with you too."

"But?"

With her body language she acknowledged she'd been caught, but she didn't admit it verbally. He kissed her in a playful way and tickled her gently.

"But what, Mariah? Don't be shy now. Be straight with me."

He gave her time to answer, not letting go and taking a chance this wasn't anything too major. He felt like a kite blowing in the strong ocean breeze. At any moment Mariah could cut the string and send him flying out of control, but he resisted the urge to take the reel from her hands. If she had something to say, he wanted to hear it, not put this off until he was in deeper than he already was.

When she finally spoke, her words were very surprising, and he didn't understand why she seemed so reluctant to ask him, or why she seemed unsure of his answer.

"Do you think I'm pretty?"

He knew what he should say and what she needed to hear, but it was obvious she didn't expect him to. Her insecurity and vulnerability did something unique to his heart. He'd been thinking about how good she was for him and how much he wanted and needed her in his life, never considering for a moment she needed him in return, or that she needed his opinion of her to be favorable. Her outer beauty and inner beauty was so obvious to him, and he knew it had to be to everyone who knew her; but she didn't know it.

"Do you remember when we went on the staff retreat last summer and we walked to that waterfall and I took a bunch of pictures?"

"Yes," she said. "You sent me some. They turned out nice."

He smiled. He'd forgotten he sent her pictures of the waterfall. That had been back in September when he needed a good excuse to write to her and he'd been trying to impress her with his photography skills. The waterfall pictures had turned out nice, but that wasn't why he was bringing this up.

"I took pictures of something besides the waterfall that day."

She appeared reluctant to believe he was talking about the pictures he'd taken of her, although he highly doubted she had forgotten. He remembered she seemed embarrassed about posing for the camera, but he thought she was very photogenic, and he kept taking shots of her, including when she wasn't aware he was doing so. The forested setting had been perfect lighting for her red hair and pale skin, and the tank-top she was wearing that day had been very flattering to her slim body and gentle curves.

"I have pictures of you from that day, Mariah. You know where they are?"

"Where?"

"On my computer."

He could see she didn't catch the significance of that. Where else would they be? Surely not anything worth printing out. He clarified what he meant.

"I made a slide show out of them and use it as my screen saver. And my favorite one has been my desktop wallpaper since Christmas."

She smiled—that embarrassed smile he loved so much. He didn't know why it had never occurred to him she would need him to tell her she was pretty, but it hadn't. He supposed it was because there was something she didn't know about him. Something he viewed as a negative trait in himself, but maybe it wasn't such a bad thing.

"I don't ask girls out I'm not physically attracted to, Mariah. I am very, very attracted to you. I think you are very pretty, and whenever we're together I catch myself staring at you all the time."

Thinking about it gave him a strong temptation to move his hands from their acceptable place on her waist to other areas on her gently curved torso and hips, but he knew he couldn't do that.

"I meant it when I said, 'Don't let me get away with anything', because you could get me into trouble really fast."

He kissed her again, feeling more on the edge of that desire than before, but also knowing he couldn't use her beauty or her insecurity about it to his advantage.

"Does that answer your question?" he asked, replacing his kisses with a hug that dispelled the lust that had begun to enter his thoughts. He didn't want to spoil this. He didn't want to hurt her or blow his chances of having her.

"Yes," she replied. "Thank you."

"Anything else?" he asked after a few moments, stepping back so he could see her eyes. If she had something to say, those green beauties would tell him so.

"No," she said, appearing content now. "That's all I wanted to know."

***

"Do you want to stop and eat somewhere before we go to the hotel?" Kerri asked.

"Yes," Kevin said. "I'm hungry."

"Me too. Do you want to go to a seafood place, or just have pizza or something?"

"Seafood sounds good. I like fish and chips."

Kerri directed him to drive to a restaurant she had been to before with her family here in Cannon Beach, and they got out of the car and went inside. He really was hungry, and it smelled good. They were seated at a table right away, and Kevin tried to focus on Kerri, not all the activity and noise around them.

That wasn't too hard for him to do whenever he was with her, but especially tonight. She was his wife now, and he felt a lot of joy in that. They were the same people, and yet he could feel a difference.

The food was good, and after a long day it was nice to be with Kerri and not have any anxiety to work his way through. Today hadn't been very stressful for him though. Once he had seen Kerri before the ceremony to have pictures taken, he'd focused on her, and the rest of the world pretty much disappeared. Even in the auditorium filled with people, he'd only seen her. Sort of like when he had a piano recital and all he saw were the keys once he started playing. Only with Kerri he didn't have to do anything except look at her.

The restaurant was close to the beach, so when they were finished eating they went for a walk down to the water as sunset approached. The waves were nice here, and the beach was wide and long. It gave him a strong sense of God's presence and power. And with the late evening sun reflecting off the water, he imagined Heaven must be something like this.

Feeling Kerri wrap her arms around his waist and lean into his chest, he remembered he often had that same kind of feeling when he held Kerri in his arms. A feeling of love so powerful it overtook his mind and heart. There was no other feeling like it, and he knew it had to be a piece of eternity. Something straight from God's heart to theirs. And something that would last forever.

They stayed to watch the sunset, and after the orange ball disappeared behind a band of thick clouds along the horizon, Kerri looked up at him, and he kissed her. He hadn't kissed her seriously since the wedding, and once he started, he didn't want to stop.

"There are no rules tonight," she reminded him.

He knew that but hadn't been thinking about it until now.

"At least not once we're alone. And I want to be alone with you, Kevin. Let's go to the hotel now, okay?"

"Okay," he said.

When they got there, he let Kerri take care of the details of checking them in and followed her lead to finding their room. They were on the fourth floor of the large beachfront hotel, and when he'd called to make the reservations, he asked for an ocean view suite, so it was pretty spacious. It had a gas fireplace and a large bathroom with both a shower and a large bathtub. In the main room there was a king-size bed, a small kitchen, a table, comfortable chairs, a large television, and it had a balcony overlooking the beach.

"Kevin, this is gorgeous," she said. "This must have cost you a fortune!"

"Only—" he started to say, but she stopped him.

"No, don't tell me. I don't want to know," she said, laughing and falling into his arms.

He wasn't sure what the big deal was. He'd been saving a lot of the money he'd been making at Tony's for as long as he could remember, and his dad had always told him, 'Save it until you have something you really want to spend it on.'

So far that had been the money he'd spent on Kerri, and on the different trips he'd taken, but even then he hadn't had to use much because his aunt and uncle had paid for a lot of it. They would be paying for most of the expenses this summer in Alaska too, but he was responsible for this week of their honeymoon and he'd never been more happy to see his money put to good use.

"I'm glad you like it," he said.

Kerri smiled at him like she wanted to be kissed, and he kissed her. He knew he could do more if he wanted to, but he felt content with just kissing.

"I think I'm going to take a bath in that huge tub," she said. "Is that okay?"

"Sure," he said. "I paid for it, you might as well use it."

She took one of her bags and went into the bathroom, and he decided to change into his pajamas. He usually wore a t-shirt and flannel pajama bottoms, unless it was too hot. But most of the time it was cool enough in Arcata for that, and it was about the same temperature here.

He'd stayed in a lot of hotel rooms before, and he always liked to sit up in bed and watch T.V., so he did that while he waited for Kerri to come out of the bathroom. There was a baseball game on he watched for awhile, but he started to feel tired and didn't want to fall asleep before Kerri was in bed with him too, so he went out to stand on the balcony and listen to the roar of the ocean. He never got tired of the sound, and it was especially loud and resonate here. He could tell the tide was coming in even though he couldn't see the water, and it was a little breezy but not too much.

The balcony had French doors that led to it, and when he heard the door open behind him, he turned around and saw Kerri standing there in the doorway, and she looked amazing. She'd had her dark hair up all day—In a fancy way with her veil at the church, and by itself on their way here. But it was down now, all wavy and styled the way she wore it on special occasions.

She also had on a beautiful white nightgown with a matching robe. The fabric looked shiny and soft and left a lot of her bare skin exposed. Especially below her neck, and her legs weren't covered. It only went halfway down her thighs.

He stepped toward her and tried to pull her into his arms, but she stepped back and pulled him inside instead. "This isn't for everyone out there to see, just you," she smiled.

After he closed the door behind him, she pulled the curtains shut, and it was then he noticed she had turned on the fireplace, turned off the television and lights, leaving most of the room in darkness except for the glow coming from the fire.

When she faced him again, his eyes fell on her, but he hesitated to go to her this time. She looked so pretty, almost too pretty to touch. He could stand here and stare at her forever.

"Do you want to go to bed now?" she asked him.

Somehow sleep was the furthest thing from his mind. "No, I want to stand here and look at you."

She smiled.

He stepped toward her then, taking her hands and kissing her fingers. "You look so pretty, Kerri. Too pretty for going to bed."

"But you've never gone to bed with me," she said. "That's a special occasion, right?"

"I guess so," he said, releasing her hands and slipping his arms around her waist. She felt amazing. So soft and exposed. Like the Kerri he knew so well and like a different one. Like his best friend and his wife.

She responded to him easily, and soon they were kissing and he was touching her like he never had before, and she was letting him without any kind of resistance. He got lost in her and forgot about everything, and he went to a place with her he hadn't known existed until now.

It was a long time before they got around to going to sleep. He learned what was so special about being married, and with as well as he thought he knew Kerri and wanted to be close to her, he didn't know the half of it.

"I love you, Kerri," he said while she rested quietly in his arms and he felt himself drifting off to sleep. "I'm going to like us being married."

"Me too," she said. "I love you, Kevin. And I'm never going to stop. I promise."

Chapter Twelve

"Good morning, Michaela."

Michaela turned and looked over her shoulder. Nick had come up behind her in the Sunday morning buffet line, and she smiled at him. "Good morning," she returned the greeting.

"How was the wedding yesterday?"

"It was nice," she said. "Beautiful and perfect. I wouldn't expect anything else from Kerri."

"You must have gotten back late. I knocked on your door at nine, but you weren't back yet."

She felt surprised he had done so, but then she remembered he had asked what time she thought she would be back, and she'd told him around then.

"I stayed to have dinner with my mom, and she had something to tell me, so it ended up being a long dinner."

She finished filling up her plate with fruit to go with her muffin and yogurt, and Nick followed her down the line and then to a table in the dining room. There weren't a lot of people here yet. Breakfast was being served from eight to nine, and it was only eight-ten.

"Do you want to share on that, or would you rather not?" Nick asked.

"On what?"

"What your mom had to tell you."

"Oh," she said. "Sure. She told me she's getting remarried."

"How do you feel about that?"

She shrugged. "I don't know. Not great, I guess. I knew this day would probably come, but now that it's here—"

He seemed to understand. They'd had a conversation earlier in the week about their families. His parents were divorced too, had been since he was five, and they were both remarried now. He had four step-siblings and two half-sisters, along with his own younger brother, and they'd been shuffled between the two families as far back as he could remember.

Her mom's marriage would give her two step-siblings. One was the same age as her and the other was older. Her dad hadn't remarried, and she'd lived mostly with her mom but had usually spent two weekends a month with her dad along with her younger sister. Jolie was sixteen and in major rebellion right now. Her mom had talked a lot about that too.

She talked with Nick about it for a few minutes until they were interrupted by others coming to join them. Adam and Lauren first, followed by Josiah and Rachael. Lauren and Rachael were both counseling, and she'd gotten to know them pretty well this week. They had all been at the wedding together yesterday. Lauren had been one of Kerri's bridesmaids, and her brother, Blake, had been a groomsman.

After she and Nick had finished eating, Warner and Mariah came to take the two remaining chairs, and Michaela smiled at Mariah. She was anxious to hear how things had gone yesterday, but she could tell by the look on Mariah's face it must have been good.

She got a chance to hear about it later after the worship-time they had together as a staff. Warner had to be in the kitchen, and Michaela caught up with her when she saw her leaving the meeting room by herself. Mariah was going to her cabin to change before lunch, and she walked with her.

"How was it?" she asked. Mariah had shared with her one day this week about her cautious optimism for her and Warner's relationship, and she'd been amazed by Mariah's patience. She didn't think she could have done such a thing, but Mariah said the wait hadn't only been worth it but also a vital part of their relationship being what Warner really needed.

"It was everything I hoped for," Mariah said. "And guess what?"

"What?"

Mariah spoke quietly. "He *is* a virgin."

Michaela smiled. Mariah had been concerned that he wasn't, and she would have been forgiving of that, but she also knew she would feel intimidated by girls in Warner's past, fearing she couldn't measure up to what they had given Warner physically.

"That's great, Mariah," she said, giving her a hug. "I'll keep praying for both of you, but I have the feeling Jesus is already on top of it."

"Yeah, He's good at that. I don't always believe it, but He keeps proving me wrong."

***

Elissa felt nervous about counseling. She remembered working on crew-team three summers ago and wishing so badly she could be a counselor, but now that she was old enough, it seemed scary.

Michaela came by her cabin to check on her before the campers arrived, and she was honest. "I don't know if I can do this. What was I thinking when I decided to come here?"

Michaela laughed and gave her a hug. "You'll do great. And if you absolutely hate it, just pretend you're sick, and I'll have to replace you."

She laughed. "Oh, great. Now if I really do get sick, you'll think I'm faking."

Her short time with Michaela made her feel better, and once her campers arrived, she fell into her role easily. All that training they'd been getting all week had prepared her, and she heard herself saying things they'd been taught to say in different situations and saw them work. This week they had junior campers: third, fourth, and fifth grade, and Dave had told them they would love their counselor no matter what, and for the most part she found that to be true.

On Monday afternoon she received a letter from Cory. She hadn't heard from him since he'd left for Europe but had expected to at some point. His letter was mostly informative about what they were doing and how he liked it. This was his second overseas trip. He'd gone to South America last year, so he'd known a lot about what to expect, but there were some differences too. Cory had in mind to possibly be a photojournalist, and she could see him doing that.

She couldn't write him back because they were moving from place to place every week. He'd told her to write him some letters this summer, telling him about what she was doing and then he would read them when they saw each other again, but she hadn't written any yet. She hadn't had time last week. She had a break now, but she didn't know what to say. So far her time here had been more about her relationship with God and admitting it wasn't what it should be. She'd known that before coming, but it was difficult to ignore here. And Cory wasn't a Christian, so anything she told him on that subject he wouldn't understand.

By Friday she was excited about going home for her dad's wedding. She missed him, and she missed home. She'd had a good week with her girls, but it was draining physically, and she felt emotionally tired too. It had been an okay year at school, but she wasn't certain she wanted to go back in the fall. She didn't have much choice, however. It was either that or stay at home and watch her dad loving someone besides her mom.

When she was away from home, she could almost pretend her mom was still alive. She missed her a lot, more now it seemed than after she first died. But for this weekend she could be happy and celebrate her dad's happiness. Knowing he wasn't alone anymore would help the separation and grief not be so bad.

Arriving at the house shortly before noon on Saturday, she found her dad in the kitchen making sandwiches. He'd been expecting her about this time, and he seemed happy to see her. They exchanged a long hug, and she started crying. She was happy for him, but the loss of her mother hit her in that moment.

"Your mom would have wanted me to do this," he said.

"I know, Daddy. I'm happy for you. I just miss her."

"Me too," he said. "I miss her every day."

***

"What would you like to do today, Angel?"

Lauren looked at Adam and spoke what she was thinking. "Be with you."

He smiled. "Doing what?"

"I don't know. What do you want to do?"

"Go to Silver Falls?"

She smiled. "What a great idea."

They hadn't been there since last summer, but once they arrived, it didn't feel like it had been that long ago. They parked in the same area, walked the same trail, and sat on the same flat rock in the middle of the gentle flowing creek. She had fallen in love with him very quickly last summer, but she'd spent the school year getting to know him. They'd had a few bumpy moments, but nothing that hadn't made their relationship stronger and all the more real.

He brought up one of those moments while they were sitting on the rock. It had been a few months since they'd been alone like this. During the weeks between school ending and camp starting, they had both been home with their families, except for when they'd gone to Amber and Seth's wedding in late May, but Blake and Colleen had been with them. And at school they had limited their time alone together to places where they had enough privacy to talk freely but could also be plainly seen by others.

They were currently in an exposed setting with other hikers walking along the creek, but she knew finding a secluded place here wouldn't be too difficult. Adam had no such intention, and she wasn't surprised, but it was good to hear his current mindset on the subject.

"I have a confession to make."

"What?" she asked. He'd been kissing her gently along with playful conversation about their time together here last summer. She was amazed by some of the little details he remembered, but she hadn't forgotten either.

"Bringing you here today wasn't a whim. I've been planning it all week. I knew we were going to have today together, and when I thought about what we could do, this immediately came to mind. But I decided I should pray about it before asking you—make sure I was strong enough to bring you here, and then Jesus started pointing out things to me that weren't just about today, but about our relationship as a whole."

"Like what?"

"Like you trusting me again. If you can't trust me on a day like today, that will spill over into other areas of our relationship. Even after we're married. Like, let's say we struggle physically but we make it to the wedding with our virginity intact, and then we think, 'Okay, that's behind us. We don't have to be strong about that anymore.'

"But that really isn't the issue. The issue is I haven't allowed Jesus to empower me to the point of complete obedience, and you've never come to trust me fully. So then, down the road of our relationship, those issues come up again. Maybe in the area of sexuality, like me being tempted to have an affair, or you always fearing that I will, or maybe in other ways, like not having complete integrity at work or you not trusting me with the ability to provide for you."

"It sounds like you and Jesus have been having some good talks."

"Yes, and He's doing most of the talking," he laughed. "It's funny how we pray about things but then He often answers in a way we don't expect. I expected Him to tell me not to come here with you today, but it was the opposite. He *commanded* me to come here and have a day like this with you. Just us. No accountability around for miles. No rules about not kissing you here or keeping everything light and friendship-focused. He said, 'You bring her here, and you show her how much you love her, and you let Me uphold you in that.'"

"And He is?"

"He is. I'm not going to be tossing all of our boundaries aside or go back to allowing my mind to see and think things it shouldn't. But I'm not going to doubt God's ability to help me in this and protect you. You can trust me, Angel, because you can trust Him."

She believed him without reservation, and he proved his sincerity throughout the day. He kissed her often, at times making her feel things she normally would view as dangerous, but they weren't. Not today. Not with Adam. Not with someone who loved her deeply and truly. Not with their Savior guarding their minds and hearts and keeping them in His perfect purity.

Purity she was beginning to see as not only about what they did or didn't do, but about who God was and how much He loved them. He had designed them to share some things now and save other things for later, and she needed to trust what God said. Maybe she couldn't understand it fully, but she could believe it.

And believing God had never steered her wrong. She always ended up right where she needed to be.

Chapter Thirteen

Nick glanced at the clock and realized it was almost dinnertime. He'd been on his bunk most of the afternoon, reading his Bible like a bestseller he couldn't put down. He did that often. Since first opening a Bible this spring, he had been caught up with several different storylines. First it had been with the people of Genesis: Adam and Eve; Noah; Abraham and Sarah; Isaac and Rebekah; Jacob and his sons; and Joseph.

Then it had been Moses and God's People in Egypt, their journey to the Promised Land, Joshua's bravery and heroics, and the time of the Judges and Kings in Israel. So far he'd loved the story of David the best. A peasant boy becoming King? He thought only fairy-tales had those kinds of plots. But it was real. A real God had led him. The same God he was getting to know.

Today he'd discovered a new character, one he had heard of certainly, but not one he'd read about yet in detail. Jesus: an ordinary boy from an ordinary family living an ordinary life until the age of thirty, and then bam! Here comes the Savior of the world. The greatest healer of all time. The greatest prophet, teacher, and miracle-worker anyone has ever seen. And He's God!

But just a man too. A man like him with flesh and blood, and weaknesses, and relationships to navigate, and friends to be betrayed by, and enemies to dodge, and decisions to make, and frustrations to feel, and victories to fight for.

He'd never thought of the Bible as being a storybook or having anything to do with modern-day life. It was straightforward and yet often forced him to dig deep, beyond the printed words. It had the answers, if he was willing to search for them.

And he was, and he was intrigued, and he could have read more, but he needed a break. He needed food, especially after skipping lunch. And he needed to see if a certain someone was here.

Leaving the guys' dorm, he went in search of anyone he could find. Elle had gone home to visit her family, and a couple of the guys he'd become good friends with were off with their girls today. But he didn't have to look too far to see people he was happy to see. Seth and Amber were sitting on the grassy bank of the lake, and he went to say hello.

"We were about to go into town and get dinner," Seth said. "Do you want to join us?"

"Yeah, maybe," he said, appreciating the invitation. "Do you know if Michaela is here? She was going shopping today with Lacey and Sara but said she would be back sometime this afternoon."

Seth and Amber both smiled at him.

He laughed. "What?"

"Oh, she was here about twenty minutes ago," Seth said. "And she was asking if we'd seen you."

"Where did she go?"

"To her room," Amber said. "She had letters to write."

"Okay, thanks. Would it be all right if I extended the invitation for dinner to her too?"

"Sure," Seth said. "We'll wait for you."

He headed for Michaela's room, jogging most of the way but slowing his pace as he ascended the stairs of the senior staff housing area. He knocked lightly on the door, and she opened it a moment later, greeting him with a smile. "You are here! I was looking for you a little while ago."

"I was in my cabin but decided it was time for dinner."

"I agree," she said.

"Seth and Amber invited me to join them, would you like to come?"

"Sure, I'd love to."

She got her purse and put on sandals and followed him onto the deck. As they descended the stairs, she asked if Elle was around today, and he told her she had gone home. They talked about her on the way up to the lake, sharing their mutual observation she was having a good summer and seemed settled and at peace about being here. They hadn't talked about her a lot before today, but enough for Michaela to know they were only friends and had been a part of each other's current journey with God.

Spending the evening with Nick, Amber, and Seth was fun. Seth and Amber were both great separately, but even better together. Seth was Nick's senior counselor, so he knew him well by now, but Nick hadn't spent much time with both of them before today, and he said something during dinner that matched her thoughts.

"Are you two the perfect couple or what?"

"I think we're doing all right," Seth said, pulling Amber close to him in the booth. "Guess where we met?"

Michaela knew the answer, but she didn't know if Nick did. He guessed right.

"It's a great place to meet the right person," Seth said.

Michaela knew Seth was teasing them, and she didn't know if Nick had any intentions toward her, but he had been rather attentive these last two weeks. They had ridden into town with Amber and Seth, so they returned to the camp the same way, but Nick asked her to go for a walk after they parted from the married couple.

Michaela told Nick what she knew about Seth and Amber's relationship when he asked. She didn't know everything, but she'd heard enough from Kerri to give him an accurate account of the major details. He said the same thing she thought often about how it was difficult to imagine coming from the families they did, being raised with God as an integral part of their lives, and being mature enough to handle a serious relationship in high school.

"I want what they have though, don't you?" she said.

"Yes," he replied. "We can't have their pasts, but maybe a similar present and future."

Michaela didn't know if he meant "we" specifically, or as individuals, but she supposed either was a possibility. She could picture herself with Nick, but she wasn't certain she was ready to get into anything heavy with him now. She was trying to figure out who she was and what she wanted, and trying to fit a relationship into that seemed like too much.

"I know this might sound weird," Nick said, "but I'm going to say this anyway."

They had reached the recreation field at the end of the trail they'd been walking on, and Nick sat on a bench that lined the edge of the large grassy area. She sat beside him and waited for him to continue.

"I've never dated anyone," he said. "In high school I had no confidence to ask girls out, and even if I had, I don't know that I would have. The girls I was attracted to in a physical sense were usually either mean or snobs, and I didn't like them.

"One of the friends I made at college this year after I came to know Christ has a girlfriend, and she's nice. If I were to date someone now, it would be someone like her. I've come up with a list in my head of qualities I'm looking for, and yet I haven't been looking. Even in coming here. I'm here to be a part of a ministry and be in a place where I can focus on getting to know God without any distractions."

He paused like he was trying to decide what to say next. She waited for him to speak his mind.

"You fit the qualities I'm looking for, Michaela. And I want you to know that. But I'm not sure if I'm ready to do anything about it."

She smiled. "I'm not sure if I'm ready for you to either."

"Really?"

"Yes. I like you, Nick. I like you a lot, but if you want to keep things as they are between us, that's fine. I'm enjoying this for what it is."

"Me too, but I'm not ruling out the possibility of it becoming more in the future. Is that okay?"

"Yes."

"And if I asked you to spend next Saturday with me, but just as a friend, what would you say?"

"I think I would say yes," she laughed. "Are you asking?"

"Yes, Michaela. I am. Anywhere you want to go, whatever you want to do. You pick."

***

Kerri gazed over the open water and breathed in the ocean air. She knew the sun was setting but couldn't see it from this side of the ship. She had been a little skeptical about a seven-day cruise from British Columbia to Alaska to begin their continuing honeymoon vacation, but having a somewhat spacious room with a balcony to step out on anytime she wanted: she could live with this. It was more like being on a moving hotel than the confinement of a tiny room with a small porthole she'd been imagining.

They'd already had a great dinner with Jenna and Caleb along with Aunt Allegra and Uncle Moshe, Kevin's wealthy relatives who were paying for all of this. And now after a couple of busy days of flying up from San Francisco and sight-seeing around Vancouver today, she and Kevin had a chance to wind down and relax. She liked being with his family, but having time to themselves was her favorite thing.

Kevin came up behind her and wrapped his arms around her waist. He'd been standing with her earlier but had gone inside to take a shower. "Are you still out here?" he asked. "It's getting cold."

"I know," she said, leaning against him for warmth. "But I like it. It's peaceful and beautiful. I could stand out here all night."

"And not sleep with me?" he said.

She turned in his arms and laughed. "It's a figure of speech. Of course I'm not going to stand out here *all* night."

"Oh, that's good," he said, giving her a gentle kiss. "Because I like sleeping with you."

Kerri enjoyed several wonderful kisses from her husband and knew she wouldn't be complaining about the cozy room they had to share, even if they'd had more spacious ones on their honeymoon. When she told Kevin the places she wanted to stay along the coast during the first week, she'd never imagined him booking such nice rooms. She knew he had money in his bank account, but she'd had no idea he would be so extravagant with it.

She hadn't been surprised by his free and loving affection. He'd always been that way, and he was still as gentle and non-threatening as ever to her previously damaged spirit. She'd often worried intimate touching from Kevin would bring back old memories of the way Jeff had taken advantage of her five years ago, but it hadn't. Kevin's touch was too different. He may be touching the same places, but he did so in a much different way.

His touch was loving and secure and pleasing, not harsh or violating, and she was falling in love with him all over again. Pulling her into their room and laying her down on the bed, Kevin stretched out beside her in his adorable pajama-wear and began giving her that tender affection, but he'd caught her in an emotional state of mind, and she began to cry.

"Why are you crying?" he asked, appearing concerned.

"I knew this would be good, but I didn't expect it to be this wonderful."

"The cruise?"

"No," she smiled, wiping away her tears. "Being married to you."

"So, why are you crying?" he said, trying to kiss away her tears, but they kept coming.

"Do you have any idea how special you are, Kevin?"

"Yes," he said in his non-arrogant, facts-of-life way. "And you're special too, Kerri."

She didn't try to argue with him or convince him he was more special than the average special person, but in her heart she knew he was.

"I'm glad God made you for me," she said instead. "And I'm glad He made you exactly the way you are."

"What am I like?" he asked, kissing her playfully.

She replied as he was kissing her neck and tickling her gently in the ribs. "You're sweet, and fun, and you always make me happy."

"You make me happy too," he said, looking into her eyes. "I've never been happier than I am now."

For as little as Kevin had known about intimacy on their first night together, he had figured it out very quickly, and as he took their playful time and turned it into something sensuous and amazing, she let herself get lost in his kisses and his touch, and she knew she'd never been happier than she was now either.

For a long time she had seen love and relationships as some kind of strategic game. Even in her careful scrutiny of guys and waiting for the right one, she'd always imagined choosing someone who fit her mold of the perfect guy and played by all of her rules. It was a good mold and they were good rules, and Kevin had measured up to her expectations—even exceeding them, and yet he wasn't anything like she had imagined either.

He was beyond reason and logic. Like a supernatural gift from Heaven that was so perfect for her, there was no game to be played. They were just loving each other, and that was the only rule.

Chapter Fourteen

Elissa had returned to camp and been in her cabin reading for about an hour when she heard a knock on her door. Inviting the person in with a call from her bunk, she saw Michaela step inside. She wasn't surprised to see her stopping by.

"Hey, how was the wedding?"

Elissa set her book aside and sat up from her reclined position against her pillows. "Okay," she said. "Kind of strange, but not too bad. It's good to see my dad smiling again."

Michaela came to sit beside her and gave her a hug. Elissa knew she could relate somewhat since her mom and dad were divorced and her mom was getting remarried, but their situations were different.

"How was your day?" she asked. "Did you see Nick at all?"

"Yes. We had dinner with Seth and Amber, and then we went for a walk here together when we got back. It was nice."

Elissa asked how that had come about, and Michaela shared the details. Michaela told her if she needed to talk more about her dad or anything else to feel free to do that anytime this week. Elissa wasn't used to being so exposed with people, but she was comfortable talking to Michaela.

She talked with her extensively on Tuesday afternoon. At first she shared the surface issues of how her week was going and how she was feeling about her dad's remarriage, but then she was more honest with something she hadn't talked about with anyone yet. Michaela knew she had a boyfriend, but she didn't know anything about him or their relationship, and it had been heavy on her mind the last few days, ever since her dad said something about it on Saturday.

She liked Cory and thought he was a nice guy. But he didn't know God and didn't seem to have any interest in church or anything religious. He knew she was a Christian, and he was fine with it. He didn't make fun of her beliefs or try to persuade her to not believe in God, but none of it was a part of their relationship.

"My dad told me I shouldn't be with him if he doesn't share my faith, and I know he's right, but Cory is the only boyfriend I've ever had, and I don't want to let go of that. It feels good to have someone, you know?"

They were in Michaela's room, so Elissa was talking without having to worry about who might overhear, and Michaela just listened. Elissa didn't know if she could relate. Michaela hadn't found that special person yet, and she hadn't dated a lot either, but that had been her choice more so than because no one was asking.

Talking with Michaela helped, but Elissa didn't feel better about it by that Saturday when she decided to write Cory a letter saying she wanted to break up and why. She didn't think she could tell him face-to-face, so she'd come up with a plan of sending him a letter that would be waiting for him when he got home. By the time she returned to school, he would know the truth and she wouldn't have to confront him if he chose to simply not come see her, or if she decided to not go back to Lifegate—something she had been thinking about off and on for a couple of weeks.

Writing the letter didn't take much effort. She told him how she felt and signed her name at the end of it. Tucking the folded stationery papers inside a matching envelope, she left it unsealed and unaddressed for now. She wouldn't have to mail it for several more weeks, but the truth was written.

She tried to put it out of her mind over the next few days, and she didn't reread the letter or open any of the ones he sent her all week. The following Saturday she went with a group of staff members to the beach for the day, including Michaela and Nick who were getting to know each other but not dating yet. She hadn't told anyone about Cory except Michaela, and she hadn't told Michaela about the letter she had written, so most of her emotions and thoughts on the subject were sitting there in her mind and heart while she pretended everything in her life was just peachy.

Michaela called her on it that afternoon when they were sitting in a pizza place waiting for the pizza to be cooked and Nick was playing video games with Warner, and Mariah had gone to watch. Elissa told her about the letter and her current plans to send it in three weeks. Michaela didn't try to talk her out of it or offer any advice.

That evening when she returned to camp, she took the three letters she had received from Cory this week, and she opened them. Reading his sweet words about how much he was missing her and how much he was looking forward to seeing her again made it difficult to imagine actually letting him go.

"Is there any hope of him knowing you, Jesus?" she whispered. "Maybe if I explained it better?"

He might know Me someday, Elissa. But you don't have to date him to make that happen. I can do it another way—In my timing, not yours. Let him go, and I will bless you for it. He's not the one I have for you, and deep in your heart you know you're waiting for someone else.

***

"Could you and Jessie have dinner with us tomorrow?" Seth asked.

Chad thought about their plans, and he didn't see why not, even though Jessie wasn't here at the moment to ask. She had gone with Amber and Colleen to see pictures of Stacey and Kenny being taken prior to the wedding.

"You're going to be in Portland?"

"Yes," Seth confirmed. "We're spending tonight at Amber's parents' house and going in to see my family tomorrow. We asked Dave for a couple of days off to see family while we're up here for the wedding."

"I'm not family," he teased.

"Close enough. You're like a brother to me."

They talked about how their summers had been going. Seth and Amber knew they had made the right decision about being at camp again this summer, and he and Jessie felt the same way about choosing to spend time with their families. Going to Disney World had been fun and problem-free in terms of getting along with his family and them accepting Jessie as a part of his life. He enjoyed the fun times he'd had with his younger siblings, and Jessie had been a part of it with him.

When it was almost time for the ceremony to get underway, Colleen and Jessica returned, but Amber was Stacey's maid of honor, so Seth sat with the rest of them. Chad kept glancing at the gold ring on Seth's hand after they were seated, and thoughts he'd managed to put on hold for the last few weeks came creeping back.

Kenny was only a year older than him—the same age he would be next summer if he asked Jessica to marry him then. Jessie would be twenty-one next summer and a year away from graduation. His excuse of them being too young to get married wasn't settling too well today.

Kevin and Kerri hadn't had dancing at their reception, but Stacey and Kenny did, and before long Chad found himself in the same situation he'd been in six weeks ago—dancing with Jessie at a wedding with all kinds of crazy thoughts and love for her overtaking his heart. He felt his heart pounding as he spoke the words, but he couldn't keep them inside any longer.

"Can we do this next summer, sweetheart?"

"What?" she asked.

"Dance—at our wedding?"

She lifted her head from his chest and looked at him. Her smile and answer came easily.

"I'd love to."

He felt emotional. For as long as he'd been putting this off and trying to talk himself out of it, he suddenly knew he couldn't take hearing her say anything else.

Moving her hand from his shoulder to the back of his hair and pulling him down for a kiss, she reaffirmed her words. "I'd love to marry you, Chad."

He didn't say anything and pulled her close, dancing with her until the music stopped. His love and desire grew exponentially during those few minutes, and he wanted to be alone with her instead of in the middle of a crowded dance floor. Leading her outside of the resort reception hall with her hand in his, he found a quiet spot and kissed her before sharing his heart fully.

"I'm scared, Jessica. I don't know if I can take care of you, but I want to, so much."

"You can, Chad, and you will."

For the moment he chose to believe her, but when he took Jessie home later and she wanted them to announce their engagement to her family, he faltered in his impulsive decision.

"I don't have a ring, Jessica. I don't want to tell them until I can give you one."

"I want to tell them," she argued gently. "I don't care about a ring, but I care about being honest with my family and sharing my joy with them. That's more important to me than a ring or anything you can give me besides your love and sincerity."

"I should have asked your dad for permission first. Let me do that sometime this week and then we can tell them."

He could see the disappointment in her eyes. He knew he was doing this wrong and letting her down. And he didn't know how to handle that. He wanted to turn and walk away, but he knew that's what his dad would have done—what his stepfather would do if his mom didn't agree with him on something: leave and escape the situation. But that wasn't him. He couldn't let himself become that.

Taking Jessie into his arms instead, he held her for a long time and confessed the real issue. "I'm sorry I'm scared. I don't want to be, but I am."

She didn't respond.

"I'm sorry I'm disappointing you," he whispered. "I'm sorry I asked you today. I should have waited until—"

He couldn't finish and started to cry. It was too much. Too much for him to handle. He loved her, but it wasn't enough. She needed more than his love. More than he had to give.

He kept holding her, but everything told him to let go and walk away. To leave and come back when he could take care of her properly. When he was done with school. When he could afford a ring. When he had the courage to face her family and say, 'I love her, and I want her to be mine for always.'

But by then she could easily move on to someone else. He could fail and never reach his goals. He could never be worthy of her. If he let go, he might never get her back. And maybe that's what he needed to accept. This wasn't right. They shouldn't be together. He shouldn't have asked her to marry him. He should tell her it's time for her to move on.

"I love you, Chad," she said.

He had stopped crying, but her words made the tears want to start again. "Jess—"

"I love you," she said again. "What does that mean to you?"

He had to think about it and came up blank. She loved him—what did that mean? Stepping back and releasing her partially, he spoke the truth.

"I don't know."

"Does it mean everything, or nothing?"

That he knew. "It means everything."

"It means everything to me too—to know I love you and you love me. It means everything. A ring is nice, but it can't add to that. I won't love you more when you can afford to buy me a ring. I love you more now when you can't afford it, but you asked me anyway. You're not asking me because you can. You're asking me because you can't not ask me."

"I'm a fool, Jessie."

She smiled. "Yes, you are. And I love that about you. This isn't about your bank account, it's about your heart, baby. A heart I love so much."

Chapter Fifteen

Gabe laid a sleeping Brittany in her crib and covered her with a soft pink blanket. She didn't stir, and he stood there, watching her. This was the first evening he had seen her since returning from Canada with his family for a week of vacation, and he had missed being here. He had missed seeing Brittany. He'd missed Sienna too.

Sienna was tired when he arrived at seven-thirty. Her mom and dad had left for their mid-summer Hawaiian vacation a few days ago, and Sienna had been on her own with Brittany for the first time. Brittany had gone to the doctor for some shots on Thursday, and she'd been really fussy ever since. He'd taken Brittany from her weary arms and hadn't minded the crying. When Sienna brought him a warm bottle to try, he had taken Brittany to the nursery, and she'd gone out in his arms ten minutes ago.

Leaving the room, he went to find Sienna and found her lying on the couch watching mindless television. He sat on the floor beside her and told her the bottle had done the trick.

"Thanks," she said.

He knew it wasn't much, considering all the times he hadn't been here to relieve her. Sienna's strength stood out to him, and he knew it had been a long four months for her—a long year. It had been about this time last summer she had told him about being pregnant. At the time it hadn't been real to him, just a problem he didn't want.

But now he didn't see Brittany as a problem, he saw her as a reality. A piece of his life he couldn't walk away from.

For the first time in over a year he'd had serious talks with God during his time in Canada. He wasn't a kid anymore. He couldn't get away with coasting along through life, trying to have as much fun as possible without thinking about the consequences of his bad choices. He hadn't been handed a bad set of circumstances; He had made them. He'd known better. He had the choices to make and had chosen poorly. He needed to admit that to himself, and he had. And now he needed to admit that to Sienna and see if they could find a solution in the midst of their messed-up world.

"Sienna?"

She looked at him and waited for him to continue.

He turned fully to face her and told her the decision he'd made this week. "I'm not going back to school next month. I'm going to stay here and work."

She didn't respond.

"I know this is where I need to be right now. Here, with you and Brittany."

She smiled, but it was a cautious smile. "I'm glad," she said. "I think Brittany missed you."

"I missed her."

Sienna didn't reply or seem surprised at his admission.

"I missed you too," he added.

She didn't say anything.

"Did you miss me, or was it good to have me away?"

"I missed you."

He reached for her hand and held it gently. "Are you glad I'm not going back to school?"

"Yes."

"I am too. Leaving was an escape for me, and I always knew it wasn't right. I don't want to run anymore, Sienna."

She let the tears fall, and he felt genuine love for her. A love he had felt for her before but had allowed to slip from his memory. Being with her hadn't only been about his physical desires as a guy, it had been about her too. About something she had done to his heart.

"I'm sorry, Sienna. I'm sorry I left you alone in this. That was wrong of me."

He kissed the fingers he was holding. Her tears continued to come, and he could see the weariness of the long day in her eyes, the failure she sometimes felt as a young mother, and the hopelessness and despair over her mistakes and poor choices.

But he could also see the joy. The joy in her prayers being answered. The joy of what could be. The joy of being loved for who she was, not what she gave to him. All along he'd been running from this because he didn't want to be trapped in a relationship he didn't want, but this made him feel free. Free to make the right choices. Free to have a second chance instead of feeling like his life was over.

"Will you forgive me, Sienna?" he asked.

"Yes," she said. "Will you forgive me?"

He answered with gentle kisses. Kisses that weren't like any he'd given anyone before. Not his previous girlfriends, or Rachael, or Sienna. Kisses of genuine caring and affection. Kisses of promise to do things right and love her even if it was difficult. He didn't expect this to be easy. He didn't expect things to always go his way. He didn't expect them to have a storybook romance. It was too late for that.

But he could love her. He could pick up the pieces of the mess he'd made, give them to Jesus, and ask Him to put it back together. It could be good like Josiah had said. Love was a good thing. Sienna and Brittany needed it, and so did he.

***

Sienna could feel a difference in the way Gabe kissed her. He wasn't being passionate and making her breathless and starting something that couldn't be stopped. He was being real.

"I want to love you, Sienna."

She knew their relationship had never been about love. She'd tried to fool herself into thinking it was, but she'd always known the truth.

"Can you?" she asked.

"Yes, I think I can. I'll be honest and say I'm not there yet. I don't know you well enough. I haven't spent enough time with you. I haven't really tried before now, but I want to."

"What about Rachael? Are you over her? If she wasn't with someone else, would you be here?"

"Yes. This isn't about not having Rachael. This is about what I really need."

"What do you need?"

"To love someone, not the *idea* of someone. I loved who Rachael was. I loved the package, but I didn't love her. If I did, I never would have hurt her like I did."

"And me? What was I?"

"An escape from my confusion. You were there when I didn't know what to do with Rachael. How to love her, or how to stop loving her."

"And now?"

He kissed her on the forehead and spoke humbly and sincerely. "You're the girl I hurt even more than Rachael, and I want to right that wrong. I can't live with myself if I don't, and I know there will be blessings on the other side if I do what God is telling me to do."

"What is He telling you?"

"He's telling me to love you. To start over and do this the right way."

Sienna felt a mixture of emotions: elation, fear, happiness, distress, uncertainty. But mostly she felt at peace. God had done this. There was no other explanation. She had surrendered herself into His hands, and now Gabe was here, but would he stay? All she could do was entrust herself to Jesus again. And only time would tell.

She fell asleep and woke up sometime later when she heard Brittany crying. She opened her eyes and saw she was alone. It was twelve-thirty. She'd been expecting Brittany to wake up one more time before she would sleep through the night—hopefully anyway. The last two nights she hadn't because of being bothered by her shots.

Pushing herself up from the sofa, she stood to her feet and headed for Brittany's room, but the light was on and Gabe was still here. He had gotten her up and was changing her diaper on the changing table. He finished up as she came to his side, and he lifted Brittany into his arms and asked if she needed to eat again.

"Yes," she said. "Thanks for staying. You could have gone."

"I didn't want to."

She took his words at face-value and sat down in the chair to feed Brittany. Gabe gave her privacy and left the room, but she didn't think he was planning to go home yet, and he didn't. Brittany fell asleep again after she finished eating, and she was able to lay her down without waking her. Going back to the family room, she saw Gabe watching a late-night talk show.

"I think I'll go to bed now," she said. "Brittany shouldn't wake up again until the morning. You can go."

"Can I stay?" he asked. "I'd rather be here than have you and Brittany here alone. The couch is fine."

"Okay." She got him a pillow and a blanket from the spare room. Once she had delivered them, she told him good night, and he let her go.

"Good night, Sienna. Sleep well."

She went to her room, changed into her pajamas, and got into bed, but it took her an hour to go back to sleep. Having Gabe here rather than being alone in the house gave her a safe feeling, but she wondered what was going to happen from here. Gabe had been coming over three or four times a week before his family went on vacation, but this was his first time here since. What were his intentions?

Her fatigue won out eventually, and she woke to Brittany's cries at six a.m. This time Gabe wasn't in the nursery when she arrived, and she took care of changing and feeding her before going out to find him asleep on the couch. She decided to do what she normally did at this time, putting Brittany into her swing while she made herself breakfast and ate at the kitchen table. Brittany was content and gave her time to read a devotion book also.

Gabe slept until Brittany started crying. She usually went back to sleep before waking in another couple of hours, so Sienna laid her down. When she returned to the family room, Gabe was slowly waking up. Sienna wasn't sure what to do. Sit down and give him a good-morning kiss, make him breakfast, or go back to the journaling she had started?

He smiled at her and sat up fully, asking what time it was. She told him, and he asked if he could take a shower. She told him that was fine, and he rose from the couch, but he reached for her before she stepped away.

"Good morning," he said, giving her a kiss on the forehead. "Did you sleep okay?"

"Yes. Thanks for staying."

"I think it's long overdue, Sienna."

He didn't elaborate on that, and she didn't comment. After he left her standing there, she went back to the table and tried to refocus on her journaling, but another thought was overtaking her heart.

I can't do this, Jesus. I can't have him and then lose him. I thought this was what I wanted, but I need to push him away. We're not ready for this. Gabe's not ready. I'm not ready! I shouldn't have let him kiss me last night. I shouldn't have let him stay.

But with her doubts and fears came the gentle words of Jesus.

Be still and know that I am God, Sienna. I'm over this. You are safe with Me. Gabe is safe with Me. This is what My grace is about. Just let it be.

Chapter Sixteen

Amber had been enjoying the summer, but it was nice to have a break this weekend. At camp she and Seth saw each other throughout the day and slept in the same bed every night, but they were sharing their first months of marriage with a lot of other people.

She hadn't realized the extra toll the leadership role was taking on their marriage until today. This was the first day they had no responsibilities and nowhere to be until tomorrow evening when they would return to camp. They even skipped church and enjoyed time alone at the house before they would be heading for Seth's house later this afternoon.

They decided to go for a walk down to the creek and have some time with Jesus together, something they hadn't been doing as much this summer as in the past. They had a tendency to want to snuggle in the morning and lay in bed for an extra twenty minutes instead of getting up. Sometimes they would find time later, but more often they had their devotion-time separately and then talked about it while they were preparing for their evening Bible study with their crew.

"I've missed this," Seth said after they'd had a good discussion about the verses they had read together. They were from Mark Four where Jesus says. *"What shall we say the kingdom of God is like, or what parable shall we use to describe it?"* They talked about how God is always looking for new ways to explain and reveal Himself. If we don't get it one way, He will try another, and He never gives up.

"I've missed it too," she said. "We need to not be so lazy in the morning."

He gave her a kiss and said, "There's value in those times too."

She agreed and supposed their relationship with each other and with God would grow in different ways at different times. They could get so focused on the ministry this summer and being diligent about having their quiet-time together they missed out on enjoying their relationship. And she'd been having personal time with Jesus during the last few weeks she hadn't felt the need to share with Seth. They were things she wanted to let rest in her heart and see how God might be leading her. And she discovered Seth had been thinking a lot about something too he hadn't shared with her until now.

"I've been thinking a lot about my career path, and I'm not certain God is leading me to be a youth pastor. I think He's wanted me to be on that path to get me thinking about how He works in people's lives and for me to be a part of things I wouldn't have been otherwise. But now that He has me where I am, I think He might be leading me in a different direction."

That surprised her, and yet it didn't. Seth had many talents and interests, and he'd never let others stick him in a box that said, 'This is who you are and what your life is about from now until you die.'

"What direction?" she asked.

"I'm not sure," he laughed. "Being a youth pastor has made sense to me because God has used me as a mentor to other high school students so much during the last couple of years, but since we've been at Lifegate it's been mostly with college guys—my peers just like before, only now they're older too. And even this summer, half of my guys on crew are out of high school. I can see myself being twenty-five or thirty and still having the biggest impact on guys around me more so than kids in my youth group."

She could see his point, and she'd experienced that somewhat too. Before going into college she had been considering youth counseling as a major because she'd been doing a lot of that in her own life, but now it wasn't so much. Even this summer with having mostly high school girls under her, they hadn't been the type to need a lot of guidance like some of the campers she'd had last summer. Instead of spending a lot of time talking with them on a personal level, she'd been letting them be, allowing God to work through the joint Bible study they all did together every night, and she'd been working on a Bible study of her own—one she was writing about her journey with God she knew could be a benefit to others.

So far her summer experience was matching up with how she felt all year at school: to continue writing whatever God gave her to write rather than having a more formal type of ministry career.

"So, I could find myself married to a doctor or engineer one of these days?"

"Yeah, maybe," he said. "Is that all right?"

"As long as it's still you."

Seth smiled and gave his wife a kiss. He appreciated her support and understanding, but he wasn't surprised by it—even in a major change. She'd always been that way. He would say, 'I think I'd like to try this', or 'I feel like God is leading me to—whatever,' and she would say, 'Okay. That's fine. Whatever makes you happy.' He was always careful to make sure it wasn't something that would be too much of a change for her or a burden, but she still had a lot of faith in him he didn't always have in himself.

"I love you, Amber," he said, laying her back on the ground and kissing her with all of the love he felt for her—which seemed to be more and more with each passing day. He had expected their relationship to be different after they were married, but he hadn't anticipated how much more he would love her. He hadn't thought that was possible, but it was.

"Do you like being married to me?"

She smiled. "I love it."

"It's nice to have extra time together today. It seems like no matter how much time I have with you, I always want more."

They spent the afternoon with her family. Ben and Hope had come for the wedding yesterday too, and it was good to have time with them, and good to see Amber enjoying her family. He sometimes worried she would miss them too much with being away from them all summer and during the school year, but she seemed to be doing all right. Along with his plans of changing his major, he wondered if a change in schools might be appropriate after next year, but he wasn't saying anything about that yet. Somehow he didn't think she would argue too much about moving closer to home, but he didn't want to get her hopes up.

They drove into Portland to meet Chad and Jessica for dinner. It had been good to see them yesterday, but he hadn't had much time with Chad. A little bit before the ceremony, but then he and Jessie disappeared during the reception.

Both Chad and Jess were smiling like he'd never seen before when they met outside the restaurant, and he knew something was up. Chad was a happy person, but he didn't get a dopey grin on his face like that very often.

"What's up with you?" he asked, giving Chad a hug and Jessie too.

"Do you want to tell them, or should I?" Chad asked his girlfriend.

"You tell them."

Chad's smile widened, and he made the formal announcement. "We're engaged."

Amber squealed and hugged Jessie, and Seth laughed at his friend. "No way. I thought you said that wasn't possible right now."

"It's not, but I asked her anyway. And I didn't have a ring to give her, but she said yes. Crazy girl."

***

Gabe decided spending the night at Sienna's house two nights in a row when her parents were out of town probably wasn't the wisest idea. Last night he'd done so because he knew Sienna was tired, and he wanted to be here to help if she had a rough night with Brittany, but Brittany seemed to be doing better today, had taken her regular naps and stayed on her eating schedule, and had just gone down for what should be a full night's sleep.

He asked Sienna if she wanted him to stay, but she said she would be all right. They had spent the entire day together, and he'd enjoyed it. One of the reasons he started spending time with Sienna originally was because she had become a friend he could talk to. He'd always liked her fine, but when he began to have thoughts and desires for her that went beyond the way he should be thinking about a girl besides his girlfriend, he'd become confused about how he really felt about Rachael. He couldn't let go of her, but he was having feelings for Sienna too. He had kissed her one night, and it had been nice, but he felt so guilty about it afterwards their relationship got messed up after that.

It had gone from being a nice friendship into something that wasn't right because he was still with Rachael, and yet he couldn't end things with Sienna either. Today had reminded him of the way they'd started out, and it was okay for him to go beyond friendship now.

He only kissed her for a little while at one point this afternoon while Brittany had been sleeping. He showed her the same caring affection as last night, but he knew it wouldn't take much to stir up desires that were difficult to control. He had never forced himself on Sienna, but when she had been willing, he hadn't been able to resist being with her.

"I had a nice day with you," he said, giving her a hug inside the front door.

"It was a nice day," she said. "Not too exciting, but this is my life."

"And I want to be a part of it," he said, knowing she needed reassurance on that. Several times today she asked if he was bored. They had mostly hung out here except to get fast food for dinner. But he hadn't been bored. He'd done a lot of thinking and silent praying and had given his old friend Josiah a call.

"I told Josiah. I can't get out of this now," he teased her, but followed his words with a gentle kiss. "And I don't want to, Sienna. I need this as much as you."

He left her on that note, drove home, and had a formal discussion with his parents about what he was thinking. He went to bed with definite plans in mind he hadn't been able to share with Sienna yet. His parents had told him all along they would help him and Sienna financially if he married her, but he'd wanted to talk more specifically with them before he mentioned that to Sienna.

He had a lot of mixed emotions as he drifted off to sleep, but mostly he felt at peace. For so long he thought he didn't want this because it wasn't anything like he had pictured living his life at the age of nineteen, but now he did want it because it was the right thing to do. Not planned. Not mistake-free. Not absent of huge challenges. But not beyond grace either.

He called Sienna in the morning. He had to work today and couldn't be there until around eight, depending on how busy the dinner-rush was, but he told her he would come over and spend the evening with her after he had a chance to take a shower and change at home, and she said that was fine.

"Do you want me to bring a movie? Maybe I won't be so bored that way," he teased her. He smiled and knew she was doing the same. "I'll miss you today, Sienna."

"I'll miss you too," she said, but he knew that wasn't easy for her to say. She was taking a huge risk trusting his sincerity on this, but hopefully she wouldn't feel that way for too much longer. Maybe a ring would convince her how serious he was.

Chapter Seventeen

Chad got off work early on Monday afternoon, and he went home to take a shower and change out of his work clothes before going over to Jessie's house for dinner. After announcing their engagement to her family on Saturday night, Mrs. Shaw had insisted on making a special dinner for the occasion, but yesterday they'd already had plans to meet Seth and Amber, so she had scheduled the celebratory dinner for tonight.

He didn't understand Mr. and Mrs. Shaw's eager acceptance of the news any more than Jessica's easy acceptance of his unplanned and muddled proposal. But he knew this is what he wanted and was glad they all supported it. He just hoped some answers to his prayers of how all of this was going to work would surface soon. At least one small confirmation from God would be helpful, but he couldn't think of anything immediate that might be waiting in the wings.

His mom was home when he got there. Sometimes he missed her if he had to work late, but he was early today and she had time before she needed to leave for the hospital. She worked swing-shift as a nurse in the ER, had been for years, and she enjoyed her work, so he expected her to be in a good mood, but she was positively giddy from the moment he arrived.

She told him to go ahead and take a shower and get changed but said she had something to give to him before she left. He'd told her and his stepdad about the engagement on Sunday afternoon while they were all at the house, and she seemed very happy for him, but her support had been a little downplayed by his stepfather's opinion of it.

Feeling curious about what his mother had for him, and not wanting to take too long, he showered quickly and met her back in the kitchen. She was waiting for him, and there was a small box in front of her on the table. It was somewhat fancy with a painted lid and Myrtlewood sides—like the kind found in many Oregon specialty shops. He didn't think he had ever seen it before.

"I keep this tucked away in a box where Walt can't find it," she explained. "It was my grandmother's, and she gave it to me years ago before she died. I don't want Walt pawning this stuff sometime when he's desperate for money, so he doesn't know about it. My grandmother's first husband was a rich man, and he was very generous about giving her nice things."

"First husband? I didn't know she was married twice."

"Yes. Her first husband died three years after they were married. He had a brain tumor. They didn't have any children together, and she had a very happy second marriage with my grandfather, so she didn't talk about him much."

She opened the box and began laying some pieces out on the table. There were several nice broaches and pins on top, and then she laid out a string of white pearls, a gold chain with an emerald pendant, and a sapphire and diamond bracelet.

"I'd love to wear this one sometime," she said, admiring the jewels she laid across her wrist. "But I'll save it for Keisha when she's older and out of the house."

Chad began to wonder if she was going to let him pick something he would like to give to Jessica as an engagement present because he wasn't able to get her a ring, but then she pulled out one last thing and held it up for him to see. It was a diamond ring, and he had no doubt it was real if his mother kept it tucked away.

"This was her wedding ring," she said, taking his hand and putting the precious piece of heirloom jewelry into his palm and folding his fingers over it. "I want you to have it and to give it as a gift to Jessica—as an engagement ring, or a temporary one, or whatever. I'll leave that up to you, but it's yours."

Tears welled up in his eyes, and he let them fall. He didn't attempt to argue with her because he knew she wouldn't change her mind, and also because he knew God had answered in a way he never expected—and many years before he had ever known to ask for it. God had provided this before he'd been born.

A gift from his mother, and a gift from his God—he couldn't turn away either.

"Thanks, Mama," he said, giving her a hug and holding her for a long time.

"I know Walt was a little cynical—more than a little cynical about the news, but I think it's wonderful, sweetheart. And I wish you all the happiness in the world. Jessica is a lovely girl, and you will be a good husband to her. I know you will."

His mother had to put the other jewelry back in its protective box and tucked away somewhere in the house for safekeeping, so he was sitting there alone within a matter of minutes, but he knew his mother's words would remain with him forever.

He was about to get up from the table when he noticed the mail sitting there unopened, and there was something for him lying right on top. Taking the white envelope with the Lifegate logo on it, he broke the seal and wondered if it might be something regarding his financial aid for this year. He was expecting it to come any day, although he wasn't expecting there to be a huge change in the amount of grant money he would be receiving since his parents' financial status had basically remained the same. He thought it might go up a little because of his other scholarship only being for his first year, but he was fully expecting the loan amount to increase more than the free stuff.

But it wasn't a complete overview of his financial-aid package. It was just a letter, and he began reading it.

Dear Mr. Williams,

After reviewing your academic record for your first year at Lifegate, we are happy to inform you that you have been selected as one of our First Year Honors students. This award of outstanding academic achievement is given to three students from each freshman class, which are selected based on overall academic performance, financial need, and deemed as students of excellence from the faculty here at Lifegate.

This award entitles you to a scholarship here at Lifegate for your second year and any successive years as long as your academic record remains in good standing. This scholarship will cover your entire balance due for tuition, books, fees, and room and board, after other grants and scholarships you may have are applied.

Congratulations, Mr. Williams. This is a high accomplishment to be proud of, and we wish you the best during your remaining years at Lifegate.

It was signed by the President of the school along with several academic deans, and a list of professors who had nominated him for the scholarship were listed at the bottom.

He felt completely overwhelmed and shocked. He didn't know such a scholarship existed or would have expected to be given one of the precious few even if he had. Holding the ring in one hand and the letter in the other, he smiled this time instead of crying.

Jesus, Jesus, Jesus! Your loving ways amaze me. Truly nothing is impossible with you. Thank you for remembering me and meeting all of my needs, even when I didn't fully trust you to do so.

You trusted Me, Chad. You may have had doubts lingering in your heart, but you've taken the steps of faith I've led you to take, and I will reward you for it.

I will always reward you for trusting Me like that. So don't stop, because many, many blessings are just waiting to be discovered by your pure and seeking heart.

***

Elle had chosen to take a break from counseling this week. It was the midpoint of the summer, and the shorter three-day camp for six to eight-year-olds was taking place along with a special family camp. Michaela had told her this was her best chance for a break if she wanted one, and she knew she could use it.

She was a little apprehensive about being under Amber and Seth's leadership for a week, but so far it had been fine. She hadn't had much contact with them since the first week and usually only saw them in passing. She didn't feel like they were ignoring her or deliberately avoiding her, and she had chosen to not bother them. This week they had been gone until this evening, and tomorrow she would be going home for a couple of days before returning on Thursday to work the second-half of Family Camp.

Being on crew had been very fun for one main reason. She had been assigned to a bathroom-cleaning crew with Nick, and they'd been having lots of fun together. He knew the jobs on crew well by now, so he'd been teaching her, but he also liked to tease her and get her to do things they didn't really have to do.

She could tell he was having a great summer without having to ask, but he told her plenty anyway, mostly related to the guys he'd formed close connections with and all he was learning about God. For her, this summer was more about her relationship with God and growing in ways she'd let slide the last couple of years. She often went home on Saturdays to have time to herself and with her family, whereas Nick was more into the group activities and was skyrocketing in his faith.

She was happy for him and didn't feel as connected to him as she had at school, but that was okay. She still didn't see him as a potential boyfriend, and she wasn't especially interested in anyone else here either. There were great guys to choose from she could probably get to know if she made the effort, but she wasn't looking right now.

Nick, on the other hand, had his eye on Michaela, which just about everyone in camp knew, including Michaela, but he wasn't totally gone on her at this point either. For now they were friends, and that was a mutual decision according to Nick. They would be going to different schools in the fall, and neither of them knew if they wanted that kind of a relationship right now, although Nick was seriously thinking about applying to Lifegate for Spring Semester of next year. From what Michaela said about the school, it sounded a lot like being here, and he knew he could use that kind of environment year-round, but he hadn't made a definite decision and was praying about it for now.

"Is there anyone else here you like?" she asked on Tuesday while they were cleaning up their mops and preparing to head for lunch in ten minutes. "Anyone on crew?"

"They're mostly younger—high school girls," he said. "But there is one counselor I've had a few nice conversations with. Can you keep a secret?"

"Sure," she said. "Who?"

"Elissa. I'm not sure what it is, but there's something about her. The last two Saturdays she's gone with me and Michaela and some others—I don't know, maybe it's nothing, but you know how you sometimes have a special feeling about someone?"

"Yeah?"

"She has a boyfriend at college, but according to Michaela she's not too set with that."

"You asked Michaela about her?"

"No, she was telling me about it. I'm still exploring things with Michaela, and Elissa will be at Lifegate this fall too, but I'm not ruling out the possibility either. Do you think I should tell Michaela that?"

"Yeah, maybe."

Elle didn't plan to say anything about it to anyone and let Nick handle his own love-life, but later in the week when she returned to work, she and Nick were working together in the kitchen along with Elissa, Mariah, and Warner. Watching Elissa and Nick together in a friendly and casual way, she could see the potential of them getting together.

She liked Michaela and thought she would be a good choice for Nick, but Elissa brought out a side of his personality she hadn't seen before, and she could tell plain-as-day Elissa had a thing for Nick—not to the point where she was being overly flirty with him or acting inappropriately, but there was something there she couldn't hide.

Chapter Eighteen

Elissa went to bed on Saturday night feeling sad about the week coming to an end. The last two days had been the highlight of her summer, but now they were over, and she didn't see them being repeated in any way in the weeks remaining.

She wouldn't be working in the kitchen with Nick again. She might have contact with him on Saturdays, but it would only be in a group situation with Michaela there too. She liked Michaela, and she had become one of her best friends this summer, but Michaela could have Nick, and she couldn't. That was the reality of it.

She refused to let herself be jealous of Michaela, and she knew it was her own fault for being unavailable this summer to any guy here, but some of those old feelings flooded her heart and mind. She wasn't attractive to guys—one of her friends was always prettier and would get asked out instead.

She told herself to accept it and not punish Nick or Michaela for the way they felt about each other. Michaela was becoming too close of a friend, and neither of them deserved it. She would mourn over the loss privately for a few days and then go on with life.

But she couldn't stop herself from replaying moments in her mind she'd had with Nick yesterday and today. They had always been around others, and yet when she was talking or working alongside him preparing food or doing the dishes, she often felt like they were the only two there. He was friendly and talked with her openly. He had a great smile and liked to tease her. He was that way with others too, but somehow he made her feel special just the same.

On Sunday morning they gathered as a staff for worship and sharing, but instead of Dave speaking for the second half of the service, he gave them time to go out on their own and have some solo time with God: asking and listening to Him about what He was saying to them at this point in the summer. Elissa spent most of the time praying about Cory.

He'd been writing her consistently, and she had been reading the letters as they came. Sometimes she felt like she could hold on and hope for things to change—to at least wait until they were at school and she could talk to him more about her faith and see if he was remotely interested in giving it a chance for himself. But if she was going to have a letter waiting for him when he arrived home, she had two more weeks to decide.

"Good morning, Elissa," she heard Nick's voice say as she was overlooking the lake. "Am I interrupting, or are you finished?"

She smiled at him and felt elated at his presence and sad about what could never be. "Yes, I'm finished," she said. "I was about to go down for lunch."

"I was heading there myself, but I saw you sitting here and thought I would check and see if you're okay. You looked deep in thought."

"Yeah," she admitted. "I have a lot on my mind today. This was good for me."

He sat on the grass beside her. "Feel like sharing, or is it just between you and God?"

She wanted to say, 'I was thinking about you.' But she couldn't. "Just between me and God, I guess."

He accepted that and didn't pry further. She asked him the same in return, and he did share something, but it wasn't very specific. "I have a couple of decisions to make. I'm still not sure what to do, but God told me to wait and He will show me at the right time."

"I know what God is telling me," she confessed, "but I'm not sure I can obey."

"Do you want to walk with me, or are you going to stay here for a few minutes?"

"I'll stay, but thanks. You gave me one more thing to pray about."

He left her then, and she was silent before God. For the last thirty minutes she had been complaining and lamenting over her woes, but now she waited for *Him* to speak. And she didn't hear Him say anything but what He had been telling her all along.

Let Cory go. He's not the one I have for you. But I do have someone. I promise.

***

Warner saw Nick sitting with Elissa along the high bank of the lake. He made a comment to Mariah who was walking beside him as they headed to lunch.

"I think he's sweet on her."

Mariah didn't argue with him. "What makes you think so?"

"The only girls I've seen Nick spend any time alone with are Elle and Michaela."

"Doesn't he like Michaela?"

"Yes, but he's not sure about it. He thinks maybe they're only meant to be friends. Maybe that's why."

Mariah looked at him and smiled. "Sometimes the one you don't notice right away is the one you're supposed to notice."

"Amen to that, sweetheart," he said, pulling her close briefly and kissing her hair. "I hope it works out as well for Nick as it has for me."

They saw them together again later while they were eating lunch. Michaela was with them along with Elle and others, and Nick seemed equally attentive with everyone at the table, but he laughed several times when Elissa spoke to him, and it was enough for Warner to ask him about it later when they were flipping burgers on the grill for a new set of campers here this week.

"What's up with you and Elissa?" he asked bluntly.

Nick smiled and didn't try to deny it. "I'm not sure yet, but maybe I'll know more by the end of this week."

"What's happening this week?"

"I need to talk to Michaela. Things are open-ended with us, but I've been getting the impression she's feeling the same way I am about just being friends. If so, I might talk to Elissa. I'm still praying about it."

"Doesn't she have a boyfriend?"

"Technically yes, but it's not something she's sure about according to Michaela."

"So, you've talked about her with Michaela?"

"No, Michaela's talked about her. A couple of weeks ago she asked me to pray for Elissa, and ever since then God's been bringing her to my mind at all hours of the day, and then I worked with her for the first time all summer this week. I think God is trying to tell me something."

"Sounds like it," Warner agreed. He'd had a similar experience with Mariah last summer. He had one date with her that didn't mean too much to him at the time, but he couldn't stop thinking about her after that. And he certainly wasn't thinking about anyone else now. He was almost certain she was the girl he was going to marry. He felt the only thing that could stop that from happening at this point was if she decided he wasn't worth her time—which he wouldn't blame her for but certainly hoped didn't happen.

He had been open with her all summer about how he felt, but that evening he decided he needed to write her a short note to reassure her of his intentions to do everything he could to keep this going between them, and share his hopes for the future of their relationship. He usually wrote her several notes each week to leave in her mailbox, but this was the most serious letter he'd ever written to her or any girl. Rereading it over after he finished, he felt his heart pounding at the words, but they were the absolute truth, and he didn't have any reason to not let her know that.

Dear Mariah,

A year ago at this time I was breaking up with yet another girl I had enjoyed dating but I didn't see myself spending the rest of my life with. It was a common pattern I wondered if I would ever break out of, but I believe I finally have. I love you, Mariah, and I believe you are the girl God has for me. For this time in my life, and for always. I can't imagine ever letting you go.

You're the first thought on my mind every morning and the last thought at night. I dream about you often—about being with you in an intimate way, and I hope that I will be someday. I've had a lot of good things given to me in my life, but you are the greatest gift from God I will ever receive. I believe you are a part of His plan for me—something He had in place before time began.

I'm enjoying this summer with you very much, and I'm not sure what the immediate future holds for us with living at opposite ends of the state and being uncertain of where the path will lead us from here, but I know we are meant to be together and distance will not separate us forever. It couldn't when I wasn't sure how I felt about you or if you were meant to be mine, and I won't let it now that I know.

Would you like to go home with me this Saturday to meet my family? You never have, and I want them to meet you. Have a great day, baby. I'll be thinking about you most of the time, and even when I'm not, you're still in my heart. Imagine a kiss from me, and I'll give you lots of real ones on Saturday. And I hope you enjoy them because I know I will.

Mariah read the letter she picked up from her mailbox after lunch, and she felt herself walking on clouds the rest of the afternoon. She was with her middle school campers most of the time physically speaking, but her heart and mind was somewhere else. With Warner and her pleasant memories of their time together this summer and what was yet to come.

She had spent the last year caring about him and hoping for things that seemed out of reach, but she had spent the last five weeks living the reality of loving him. She loved loving him. He was easy to love and a challenge to get close to at the same time, but somehow she was doing it.

She missed him during the week, but their little notes to each other usually kept her going until she could have time with him on Saturdays. By Wednesday evening, however, she couldn't stand to not see him for another three days. She felt a little ridiculous about it, but she went to Michaela after dinner.

"Could you find out what Warner's schedule is like tonight and if we might possibly have a break at the same time? He's been working on that new water line all week, and I haven't seen him since lunch on Sunday!"

Michaela laughed, but she granted her request. Twenty minutes later before the evening meeting for the campers began, she told her what she'd found out.

"He has a break from eight-thirty until lights-out at ten. The kids have their snack break from eighty-thirty until nine before Fireside tonight, so if you go up to the staff lounge then, he should be there. I told Seth to let him know."

"Thanks," she said.

"Seth also told me he's trying to talk Warner into counseling for high school camp next week, and he would appreciate any influence you could have on that."

She laughed. "Okay, I'll try."

Eight-thirty was only two hours away, but it seemed like an eternity until recreation time ended and she was on her way to the staff lounge. She couldn't stay for the whole half-hour because she needed to change into warmer clothing for campfire time, but twenty minutes would be better than nothing.

He was waiting for her outside the door, and she slowed her pace when she saw him, but he'd already caught her running, and he couldn't resist teasing her.

"Who are you in such a hurry to see, Rose Petal? You look out of breath."

She stepped into his arms and enjoyed a long hug without feeling the need to explain.

"I've missed you too," he said seriously before releasing her and stepping back to look into her face and give her a gentle smile.

"This has been the longest week. Where have you been?"

"In the forest mostly. We're trying to get this ditch dug by next week when several of the guys will be needed for counseling."

She smiled. "I heard you might be one of them."

He shook his head. "Oh no, not you too. Did Seth arrange this little meeting?"

"No, I requested it, but there might be a price to pay. Sorry."

"It would be all right, I guess. I'd see you more, if nothing else."

"You never know, you might have one of those guys in your cabin who can't seem to find the right girl but is most eager to try. You could tell him to keep searching until he finds her."

"Thanks for your note today," he said, pulling her close again. "When I didn't get one yesterday I thought maybe I'd said too much."

"No," she assured him. "It took me a day to figure out what to say back. I've never gotten a letter like that before."

Neither of them said anything for several minutes while he held her gently in his arms. She felt closer to him than she ever had before, and she didn't feel afraid of it going away. Warner could easily have any girl here, but he'd chosen her, and after all of her waiting and prayers, she felt very secure in that. God hadn't just done this for her, He'd done it for Warner too, and He wasn't going to let them down in what He had started.

Telling her he loved her in the letter had been the first time Warner had said that, and she was hoping he would say it out loud this Saturday when they went to see his parents, but he didn't make her wait that long.

"I love you," he said simply, breaking the silence but not releasing her yet. "Do you love me, Mariah?"

"Yes," she replied.

"Don't stop, okay? I don't think I could take it."

"I won't."

"Could you meet me tomorrow before breakfast?" he asked.

She stepped back and looked at him. She'd suggested that once during her first week of counseling, and he said something about not wanting to be that obsessive about needing time together. She hadn't mentioned it since.

"I know, it's a little obsessive," he said. "But I want to be obsessive about you."

She smiled. "I guess I could make an exception."

"I appreciate your patience with me, Mariah. It's taken me awhile to figure out how to love you and be loved by you, but now that I'm here, I know there's no other place I'd rather be. When I'm loving you, my heart feels completely at peace—like that's what it was made to do."

Chapter Nineteen

Nick saw Mariah and Warner standing together outside the staff lounge, and he watched them from a distance. He knew from talking to Warner that he was in love with her, and their interaction together now certainly supported that.

Watching them also supported his own feelings about Michaela. He liked Michaela a lot. He thought she was a wonderful person with a great personality and someone he enjoyed being around and talking to, but that's as far as it went. He couldn't imagine looking at her the way Warner was looking at Mariah, and he didn't think she would ever look at him that way either.

He knew this was the time of day he would have a good chance of finding her, and he took the back trail to the main camp area. When he didn't see her in any of the main buildings, he went to her room and knocked on the door, and she opened it.

"Hi," she said in her bubbly way. "This is a surprise."

"I was thinking about you and had a break, so I thought I come see if you were busy. Are you, or could I have a minute of your time?"

"I'm free. Just waiting for bedtime when I get to make sure 100 middle school girls are where they're supposed to be for the night."

"You're having too much fun this summer," he said, thinking of how he'd been digging a ditch all day and breaking his back. He wasn't used to that kind of heavy-duty labor.

"I know," she said. "And to think I was worried this was going to be a tough gig."

They chatted casually with one another for a few minutes like they usually did whenever they saw each other. Even when they spent time together away from camp on Saturdays, this was mostly how they'd spent their time. Just talking and laughing together and enjoying their friendship. The times they had talked seriously, it was either about God or their families, not anything related to their relationship with each other.

"I have something I need to say," he said when there was a break in the conversation. He told her he'd enjoyed the time they had spent together this summer and didn't want that to change, but he also felt he needed to let her know he wasn't looking for anything beyond what they already had.

"I feel that way too," she said. "I like you, Nick. I like talking to you, and you've been a good listener and a good friend to me these last several weeks, but I think that's as far as I want this to go."

He gave her a hug, and it was nice. He hadn't been able to hug many people in his life, and it reminded him how he'd made so many friends this summer who were so different from any friends he'd ever had before.

"Can I ask you something?" he asked.

They released each other, and she answered him. "Sure."

"Do you know anything new about Elissa and her boyfriend since the last time we talked about it?"

She smiled. "Oh? Why would you be wondering about that?"

"Just curious," he said but didn't do a great job of hiding his real motive. "I mean, you did ask me to pray for her, and I—"

"Yeah, yeah, save your breath, Romeo," she laughed. "But seriously, it's funny you should mention that."

"Oh?"

"I hadn't talked to her about it for a couple of weeks, but she came to me this afternoon and said she made a final decision."

"And what decision is that?"

"She wrote Cory a letter, telling him she can't be with him because of their different beliefs."

"How is she going to send it to him?"

"She'll send it to his home address, and it will be waiting for him when he gets there in two weeks."

He didn't say anything.

"So, you like her, huh?"

"Yes," he said. "I hadn't had any time with her except when she's been with us, but we worked together in the kitchen last week, and I don't know, there was something about her. Something that even though I was still thinking about us and wondering where that was going, and I knew she had a boyfriend at school, I still kept smiling every time I saw her and wishing she was around when she wasn't."

This time Michaela didn't say anything.

"Would that bother you—if I asked her out? I know you two have gotten to be good friends this summer, and I wouldn't want to get in the way of that."

"No, it's fine," she said. "I think that could be a really good thing for both of you. Don't let me stand in your way."

"Has she ever said anything about me?"

She laughed. "No, but if she likes you, I think I'd be the last person she would tell. She did say several times she thought you were really nice and that she hoped it worked out for us, but I'm not sure I believe that."

"Don't say anything to her. I'm still praying on it, but I wanted to make sure you were feeling about me the way I was feeling about you, and see if you knew anything about her and Cory."

"Now you know," she said. "But how do you feel about the distance-thing? You kept saying you weren't too sure about that with me."

"I don't know. I guess I'm not really thinking about it."

"Distance is a good test for a relationship, and some of them do pass it."

He thought again of Warner and Mariah. "Yes, some of them do. Maybe we'll get lucky that way too—If I end up asking her."

"And if she mails that letter," Michaela added.

***

Elissa opened her Bible to begin her evening devotions with her camper girls before lights-out, and she took the envelope from the pages that had marked her place. She was planning to share something from her time with Jesus this morning as a way to end this day with her girls, and she had placed the letter to Cory there because she knew it was time to send it.

The words of Jesus along with her talk with Michaela this afternoon had confirmed what she'd been hearing God say to her, and it was a disappointing prospect for her to let go of her first boyfriend, but she knew it was a step of faith she needed to take.

After sharing things with her campers along the same lines, she turned out the light and had a private prayer time about possibly mailing the letter tomorrow morning. It was addressed and had a stamp on it. All she had to do was take it with her when she went to the morning counselor meeting and drop it in the outgoing mailbox on her way past the camp office.

But it was scary, and she didn't know if she could do it. She didn't like the thought of not having a boyfriend when she returned to school and having to be set up with all of Abby's choices for her again. That's how she had ended up with Cory, and the guys Abby always found for her either weren't Christians, or they were but weren't serious about their faith. She wanted a guy who was: someone like Nick and other guys here, but she didn't know how to attract them.

And there was the possibility Cory could become like them. If she made a serious effort to talk to him about Jesus, what He meant to her, and how He could make a difference in his life too, she knew there was a chance he would surrender his life to God. She believed in God's ability to do that, and she hadn't honestly tried to share her faith with him.

But there was the clarity of God's voice to consider above all else. He was telling her to let go, and she knew it. Maybe Cory would encounter God at some point, but she wasn't the one to lead him there, at least not as his girlfriend. She hadn't always listened to God's voice when she knew He was leading her a particular way, and it had always ended in heartbreak or disaster. And coming here this summer was one of the things she had said yes to, although somewhat reluctantly, but it had turned out much better than she expected.

She was living in a different world here. One away from her life at college this past year with Abby always manipulating and controlling her, going out with a guy who was nice but she couldn't connect with on an emotional or spiritual level, and feeling clueless about what she wanted out of life.

Her circumstances here weren't exactly the way she wanted them to be either, but her faith had become much more real, and God was drawing her close to His Heart. She could feel it, and she needed it.

If she didn't trust Him in this, she doubted she would ever fully trust Him in anything, and then where would she end up? She shuddered to think of the possibilities. She had seen enough of Abby being in and out of negative or meaningless relationships to know she wanted something different for herself.

In the morning she felt braver than she thought she would, and taking the letter and dropping it into the slot wasn't too difficult. It was on her mind during most of the counselor meeting, but after that she went about her day, and it only came to mind a few times.

She didn't get a letter from Cory that day, so that helped, and then after dinner when Michaela caught up with her and asked how she was doing, she told her about mailing the letter, and Michaela was supportive of her decision. She accepted her hug and cried a few tears, but she felt at peace and trusted God to carry her on from here, just like He promised.

***

Sienna felt Gabe take her hand in the cool evening air, and she felt familiar tingles at his touch. For the last two weeks he had been showing her gentle affection freely whenever they were together, which had been every evening and the better part of the day when Gabe didn't have to work. His efforts to be with her and make their time together meaningful surprised her but seemed genuine, not forced. She didn't feel like he was doing any of this because he had to, but because he wanted to.

Their evening walks had become a habit with the sunny and clear days they'd been having in mid-July. It didn't get dark until after nine o'clock and was warm enough to be outside. This was Brittany's nap time before her last feeding of the day, so they could leave her at the house with her mom and dad while they went out to have more privacy than being in the house allowed.

Gabe kept coming back day after day, and with him not working today and being here for about nine hours now, he didn't seem anxious to go home earlier than usual. They'd gone to a matinee movie this afternoon and had a quick dinner together afterwards before returning to the house, but otherwise they'd just been hanging out all day—being children under her mom and dad's roof and parents at the same time. It was strange. She knew she would enjoy them getting out on their own eventually, but she also knew that wasn't possible right now. She would have to find a job to make that work, and she didn't feel ready for leaving Brittany all day.

Gabe walked a few more paces with her hand in his before he stopped and pulled her close to him. Without saying anything, he kissed her gently several times, and he seemed more deliberate about it than normal, like he had a specific reason for kissing her.

"Do you remember the first time I kissed you?"

"Yes," she said without having to think about it.

"The way I kiss you now reminds me of that."

"Is that good?" she asked, not knowing how he felt about their first kiss. It hadn't been right because he was dating Rachael at the time, but she remembered it as being a very good kiss. Something pure and innocent in a physical sense, just wrong because of the timing.

They had been friends, and they'd done simple things like working on their homework together at the library before going home for the evening and meeting each other at the movies on Saturday night or Sunday afternoon. She'd gone to watch his basketball games, and he dropped by the ice cream shop on the evenings she worked there, and he called her on her cell phone when she was at home and they would talk for an hour. She'd had a crush on him, but he didn't know that. She hadn't coerced him into kissing her the first time. He'd done so on his own one Saturday night when he was telling her goodnight beside her car after they'd seen one of their favorite movies for the third time.

"Yes, that's good," he said, kissing her again in the same way now, and she knew what he meant. It was like their first kiss but without the guilt afterwards.

"I knew it was wrong, Sienna, but I enjoyed kissing you. You were a good friend to me, someone I could talk to, and I was attracted to you—I just had another girlfriend at the time, and I wasn't sure what to do about that."

She didn't know what to say and he continued.

"I chose poorly, and I'm sorry I hurt you."

She thought he was going to say, 'I never should have kissed you,' but he said something else.

"I should have ended things with Rachael then or before I started something with you. I hate to say I was a stupid kid and let that be my excuse, but I was. And I knew what I really wanted, but I was afraid of it."

"Afraid of what?"

"Loving you. But I'm not afraid anymore. You're easy to love, Sienna. I just went about it the wrong way."

He held her close, and she didn't expect him to say anything else. Gabe talked a lot, but he didn't usually express his feelings or anything too deep like this. But he wasn't finished.

"I love you, Sienna, and I want us to get married. I know it won't be easy on our own, but I want it. We're not kids anymore, and I think we need to be the adults we've forced ourselves to be. It might not be easy, but it will be right."

She didn't have the strength or a good enough reason to argue with him. "When?" she asked.

"Soon. In a few weeks if you want."

She stepped back and was honest with him. "I don't know if I want to start working again yet."

He smiled. "You don't have to. My parents are going to help us out. Whatever we need for rent and food and bills that my job doesn't cover, they'll make up the difference."

"You talked to them?"

"Yes. They've always wanted me to marry you, even if I didn't love you, but I do, Sienna. I really do, and I'm sorry I lost sight of that. I'm sorry I didn't show you in the right ways when I knew it, and that I forgot why I ever kissed you in the first place."

He took a ring out of his pocket then, and he reached for her hand. "Will you marry me, Sienna? Will you let me make this right and love you again—for the rest of my life?"

"Yes," she whispered.

He put the ring on her finger and pulled her close. "God's grace, Sienna. It makes all things possible. It's a real thing, and I want us to live it together. And I've honestly never wanted anything more."

Chapter Twenty

Josiah took the printout of the email that had been placed in his mailbox, and he read the message Gabe had sent to him. Since Gabe had called him two weeks ago, he'd been having high hopes his friend was finally coming around, and he had been praying for him every day, but it was good to see Gabe wasn't going about this halfheartedly. They had set the wedding date, and he wanted to know if he would be his best man.

"Who's that from?" Rachael asked.

They had met here for their afternoon break time, but Rachael had been reading her own mail. He let her read the message for herself. She let the tears fall as a smile emerged on her face. Josiah gave her a hug, or maybe she was giving him one. It had been a long road for both of them in different ways, but this was the outcome they had been hoping for.

Neither of them said anything. It didn't need to be said. Josiah had been having a great summer as a camp counselor, and he'd been enjoying time with Rachael when they could find it, but this really made his summer complete. The one thing he had prayed for so often but honestly didn't know if he would ever see.

Rachael had her own news to share. Not something so life-changing, but something exciting nonetheless. Her wedding dress was in. She had ordered one in May, and it had arrived at the shop for her to try on and see what alterations needed to be made. They weren't getting married until December, but since they were going to be in California this fall, she was trying to get as much done now as possible.

"Do you want to go home tomorrow and do that?" he assumed.

"Can we?" she asked. "My mom said to call and she would make an appointment."

"If you want."

"Hearing about Gabe makes me more excited for our wedding," she said.

"Why is that?"

"When other people are going through difficult times and I'm not, it sometimes makes me feel like I'm living in a dream-world that can't possibly last. Like me and you are just happy in our relationship because we don't have any major struggles right now. But Gabe and Sienna are happy now, and they still have a lot of challenges to face. They aren't getting married because there's nothing stopping them. There is, but they're doing it anyway."

He knew what she meant, and he felt that way too. He honestly hadn't made any huge mistakes in his life. A few wrong choices here and there but nothing life-changing or something to hold him under a cloud for a long time.

And now here he was, just four months away from marrying the love of his life, and he sometimes couldn't help but wonder, 'Okay, when is the bomb going to drop? When am I going to wake up and realize my picture-perfect life has just been a fairy-tale that can't last forever?'

At about that same moment they saw Seth and Amber come in the door to check their own mailbox, and they all greeted each other and asked how their days were going. Josiah told them the news about Gabe and Sienna, and they reacted the way he expected. He actually hadn't seen Amber and Seth together much this summer. Usually just on Sundays and once in awhile during the week, and he decided to ask them something that could be seen as a casual conversation question, but he was asking it because he seriously wanted to know the answer.

"How's married life, you two? Everything you hoped it would be?"

Amber and Seth looked at each other and smiled. "It's even better than I expected," Seth said. "How about you, sweetheart?"

"Yes," she said. "I don't think we could have known what it would really be like until we were married, but I'm not surprised I'm enjoying it. I've always enjoyed everything about our relationship."

Josiah turned to Rachael and winked. "I guess we'll be finding out about that soon."

"I can't wait," she said.

Josiah knew she meant that, but he had a difficult time believing a beautiful girl like Rachael wanted to be with him. She could have any guy here, or anywhere, and she was choosing him?

"You're crazy," he said. "I think you should have shopped around a little more before you settled for me."

"Oh, no," she said. "I've seen quite enough of the other kind of guys to know you're the kind us girls should be looking for. Right, Amber?"

"Absolutely," she said. "I found mine, and you found yours."

The following morning when they were headed for Rachael's house, Josiah asked her something their conversation the previous afternoon had made him wonder.

"Do you think it could have really been for you and Gabe—if he would have made different choices when the two of you were together, or do you think he was meant to be with Sienna all along?"

"I think he was meant to be with her."

"Why?"

"I never realized it until I was with you, Josiah, but what Gabe and I had—and what Steven and I had—was based on both of us being confused about what real love is and then assuming we had it because we were happy being together. But there was no depth. No real concern for the other person and a dependence on each other. I liked Gabe. I thought he was a nice guy, and we had fun together. I liked Steven. We both had needs we were able to fill for each other for a time. But it wasn't love like the way I love you."

"How do you love me?"

"Like my life would never be the same without you. Losing you wouldn't just be a disappointment or change how I spend Saturdays—It would leave a void that no one else could fill."

He thought about his love for Rachael, and he hadn't realized it at the time, but back when he first began calling Rachael and writing to her and sending her those daily messages, he'd been giving her his heart in a way that was both scary and also impossible to not do. If he contacted her, he would think, 'I hope she was happy to hear from me. I hope it made her day.' And if he didn't, either because of busyness or fear of rejection, he would think, 'I should have called. I let her down.' He couldn't even imagine doing anything to hurt her now and then not making it right. To not show her love would suck the life out of him.

"Do you love me, Josiah?" she asked.

He realized he'd been silent and could see how not responding to her definition of love could make her doubt that, but he knew she had no reason to.

"I love you, Rachael. I love you very, very much. No worries."

***

Nick had been debating all morning about asking Elissa out today. He wanted to and felt like God was answering his prayers with a solid yes, but the cautious side of him wanted to wait a week just to be sure. He had heard from Michaela that she'd sent the letter to Cory, but maybe this was too soon for him to be pouncing on her after such a serious decision. Maybe he would be getting her on the rebound, or maybe she needed some time to herself. He didn't want to be an annoyance or turn what could be a carefree day for her into a stressful one.

He continued to debate about it all through the final staff meeting before they were dismissed for their day off. She was on the opposite side of the room in the large circle they always formed facing one another with Dave in the middle, thanking them for their hard work for the week and reminding them of what was to come tomorrow. He was going to be counseling for the first time because they needed all of the college-age guys to step in for high school camp, and he was nervous about it. Why add a stressful thing like asking a girl out and possibly having it be a disaster?

Glancing at Elissa several times, he kept missing what Dave was saying. She looked subdued, and he knew the reality of what she had done was hitting her. Was she wondering if she had made a mistake? Had she? Or could she use a fun date and someone to talk to today? Would a date with him bring a smile to her face, or would it make her day worse?

Michaela caught his eye, and she smiled at him like she knew exactly what he was thinking. Michaela thought he should go for it, but he wasn't so sure. He saw Michaela turn and say something to Elissa, and Elissa smiled a bit. He didn't think Michaela had said anything about him. He'd asked her not to step in and play matchmaker, but a few moments later Elissa did look right at him and caught him staring. He smiled without effort, and she returned it, but as soon as she looked away and refocused her attention on Dave, her sad face returned.

Dave prayed for them before letting them go, and Nick was praying the whole time for his own immediate concerns. *Okay, Jesus, what am I supposed to do? I think I'm going to ask her, but if I shouldn't, please tell me no.*

He didn't hear any such answer, and as soon as Dave finished, he began walking toward her. With every step his heart pounded harder, but he managed to make it all the way to her side without changing his mind.

Michaela was walking with her as they were making their way out of the dining hall, and he said hello to both of them casually. He hadn't talked to either of them today. He'd been working in the kitchen all morning.

"Hi, Nick," Michaela said, turning to give him a hug. "Where were you working this morning?"

"In the kitchen," he said. "How about you?"

They both laughed. He liked to tease her about her schedule that was very random and didn't have specific duties like working on crew or being a counselor. Her role was more people-oriented, so she often stood around feeling like she didn't have anything to do, but in reality she was on-call twenty-four hours a day, always needing to be available and ready for whatever came up that needed her attention, a listening ear, or a decision on.

"What are your plans for today?" he asked, trying to convey he was asking both of them.

Michaela spoke first. "I'm going into town with Seth and Amber for lunch. We're planning something for next week I can't tell either of you about, and we need to plan it and then pick up stuff at the store. After that—I don't know. Probably just hang out here. How about you, Elissa?"

She shrugged. "Not much, I guess. I need to do my laundry."

"There's Amber," Michaela said, looking over her shoulder. "I'd better ask when they're planning to leave."

She left them standing there together, and Nick could see that Elissa wasn't thrilled at the prospect of a whole Saturday before her with nothing to do, but she had the courtesy to ask him what his plans were.

"Actually," he said, stepping a little closer and lowering his voice for her ears only. "I was thinking of talking to you about that. Can we go outside for a minute?"

She stared at him. He stepped past her and said over his shoulder, "The door is this way."

She followed him across the room, and he held the door open for her. They both stepped onto the deck, and he led them to the railing. Elissa didn't utter a word the entire time.

"I heard you sent a letter to Cory this week."

She appeared surprised he would know that. "Did Michaela tell you?"

"Yes, but only because I asked."

"Why would you ask her about that?"

"She asked me to pray for you a few weeks ago, and I was curious if you had made a decision."

"Oh," she said like she considered that to be a good enough reason for him to know, but not like she thought he cared that much about her personal life. "I've been praying about it all summer, and I know it's the right thing. I've always known, I suppose. It just took me awhile to listen."

Her words went straight to his heart. He knew what God was telling him to do. He needed to listen and obey too.

"Would you be interested in spending the day with me?" he asked. "Maybe do something a little more fun than hanging around here and doing laundry?"

She stared at him.

"It can just be a friend-thing if you're not ready to start dating someone else this soon, or if you want to say no, that's okay too. I was just wondering."

"Did Michaela tell you to ask me?"

"No. I did ask her if it would be okay with her if I asked you out, and she's fine with it. Did she tell you we decided to just be friends?"

"Yes."

"Do you want time to think about it? I know this is probably a little surprising for you, but I enjoyed working in the kitchen with you last week, and you've been on my mind ever since."

Chapter Twenty-One

A little surprising? Up until yesterday I thought you were dead-gone on Michaela. Why would you go out with me?

Elissa didn't need any time to think about what she wanted to say, but should she? She could only recall two other times she had felt this excited about someone asking her out—someone who was asking because he wanted to, not because someone else talked him into it; but so far her other two promising prospects hadn't turned out so well.

There was Cory, of course, who had surprised her after their first double-date with Abby and one of his friends. They'd had a fun time, and she didn't have any reason to say no when he said he'd like to take her out again sometime. And their relationship had been very pleasant for what it was.

The other guy was Adam. He'd asked her out during her first summer here, and it had been a dream-come-true for her. But she had either misunderstood his intentions, or he'd decided he didn't like her after all. He claimed the first was true, and she could see how she may have read more into his words than he actually said. She didn't think she could be misreading anything with Nick, but even if he was asking her on a date, would he actually enjoy it? Like he said, they didn't really know each other, but she had been secretly admiring him all summer, and denying that would be foolish. She couldn't afford to waste opportunities like this.

"I'd like to spend the day with you," she said, trying to sound excited about the invitation but not too excited. "Thanks. This has been a tough week, and I wouldn't mind getting away today and having fun."

He smiled. "Where would you like to go?"

She shrugged. "Doesn't matter. What were you thinking?"

"The beach."

"Okay," she said, feeling more shocked by his suggestion than she let on.

"Just one thing," he said.

"What?"

"I don't have a car here. Do you mind driving?"

"No, that's fine."

"I'd pay for the gas."

She didn't really care either way because she used her dad's credit card for buying gas, but she appreciated the gesture. "And you can drive, if you want," she said. "Or I will. It doesn't matter."

"I will if you want me to," he said in a caring way. "This has been a long week for you."

"Yes," she admitted. "I woke up this morning feeling like I really wanted to drive home and see my mom and talk to her about my decision, but—"

She couldn't finish her thought, and she didn't have to. Nick knew about her mom's death and her dad's recent remarriage. She had talked about it when she'd spent part of a Saturday evening with Michaela and Nick, just the three of them. She had found them both easy to talk to that night, and they'd both expressed sympathy for her loss and difficult changes. They each had their own, so she felt like the three of them had a lot in common, and it had been her favorite time of the summer so far—a time when she had been completely herself and accepted for it.

Nick didn't seem bothered by her honesty now either. "For what it's worth, I think you made the right decision about Cory—from what I heard from Michaela, anyway. And if you want to talk about it today, that's fine. But you don't have to."

"That could go either way," she admitted, not feeling like she knew if she wanted to talk about it or not, or if she would be comfortable doing so with him. She laughed. "If you don't mind which way, then let's go."

They separated briefly to get what they would need for the day, and she met him back at the dining hall ten minutes later. She thought about trying to see if Michaela was still here and telling her where she was going, but she decided not to. She trusted Nick, and she felt like this was only about them and she didn't need to involve anyone else. She didn't even care about others knowing she had a date for the day. Just having Nick waiting for her when she returned was enough.

They walked to the staff parking area together, and they saw Elle when they arrived. She was getting into her car, and Elissa hadn't been thinking about her and Nick being friends until they saw each other. But it was obvious from Nick and Elle's exchange that Nick knew Elle was planning to go home today, and that Elle knew of his plans to ask her out.

"This guy is the sweetest and most generous person I have ever met," Elle bragged on him. "And the best listener. You are in for a real treat today, Tinkerbell."

Elle always called her by her camp name because they were usually around campers when they saw each other. She hadn't gotten to know Elle all that well, but she knew one thing about her: she was even prettier than Michaela.

"What's with you having these beautiful girls as friends?" she asked after they were in the privacy of the car. "Do you have a policy about not dating beautiful girls?"

He looked at her and smiled. "Obviously not."

She smiled at his sincere compliment, and somehow he made her believe it. Within minutes they were cruising down the mountain on the winding road through the forest, and she laid her head back against the seat and closed her eyes. Nick was quiet for several minutes, and she tried to figure out how this had happened. What was he doing?

He reached over to touch her cheek, and it was a pleasant feeling. Nick had a very sincere quality to him. He didn't flirt with girls or play games. He liked to tease, but in an attentive, caring way, not an obnoxious one. She couldn't recall a single time he'd made her feel stupid or embarrassed. And she also couldn't recall him ever showing another girl this kind of caring touch. Hugs yes, but not anything of an intimate nature.

She opened her eyes and smiled at him.

"So, is this a date, or just a friend-thing?" he asked. "I'm fine with either, but I'd like to know what you would like it to be."

"I'd like it to be a date," she said. "But if at the end of the day we change our minds, I want us to still be friends. You and Michaela have been my best friends this summer, and I don't want to let go of that."

"Michaela *and* me?" he asked.

She reminded him of that evening they'd had dinner together in town, just the three of them. "That was a very special time for me. I needed it a lot, and the two of you were there for me. It was like all the good talks I've had with Michaela, only better. I'll never forget it."

***

"Hey, Gabe. What's up, man?"

Gabe laughed and didn't feel surprised to be hearing from Josiah today. He was hard to reach at the camp, and Gabe had decided to just send him an email, but he knew Josiah wouldn't be satisfied with that.

"At the moment I'm talking to you with one hand, and I've got my baby girl in the other arm. What are you doing?"

"Sitting in the car outside a wedding dress shop while Rachael is getting fitted for her dress."

Gabe laughed again. "Good to hear from you," he said. "I assume you got my message."

"Yes. That's great, man. I'm proud of you."

"And I'm indebted to you for life. You saved the day for both of the girls I've ever cared about."

Josiah didn't respond to that, and Gabe didn't expect him to. Josiah wasn't one to gloat or take credit for anything, even if he had every right to.

"So, how about it? Will you be my best man? That's the weekend you're going to be here, right?"

"Yes, that's the one, and yes, I will, Gabe. Where are you getting married?"

"At the church. Your dad is doing the ceremony for us, and we're just having a simple reception afterwards. Nothing fancy, but real. That's all we need."

They talked for awhile longer about where they were planning to live and that he was going to keep working for now, and Josiah was supportive of everything he had to say.

"You know what I remembered?"

"What?" Josiah asked.

"I remembered the reason I ever kissed Sienna in the first place was because she had become my best friend."

"I know that feeling," Josiah said. "You'll be my best man too, right?"

"You haven't already asked someone?"

"No, I was holding out, hoping for a miracle."

Sienna had been in the other room, but she came into the nursery and didn't have to ask to know whom he was talking to. She took Brittany from him because she was ready to eat. She wasn't looking to interrupt their conversation, but Gabe got up from the chair and pulled her back to him before she could leave the room. He kissed her while Josiah was saying something about when they were going to be coming up next month.

"Are you listening to me or kissing your fiancée?" Josiah laughed.

"Hold on a sec," he said into his phone and then spoke to Sienna. "Will you go out with me tonight?"

She smiled and said yes.

He had only arrived twenty minutes ago while Sienna was in the shower, and he hadn't talked to her yet today. Normally he worked on Saturdays, but he'd gotten today off so he could spend the day with her and take her out for an engagement dinner. She already knew that, but it was fun to remind her of what was to come.

"You're hopeless, man," Josiah laughed at him. "You always were the ladies' man. Much more charming than I could ever hope to be."

"Yes, but this time it's all for her. And that isn't how I got her. I won her heart by doing exactly what you told me to do."

***

Standing in front of the mirror, Rachael let the tears fall softly onto her cheeks, and she wasn't too quick to wipe them away with the tissue her mother handed her.

It wasn't so much the dress that made her cry, as it was the man she was going to be wearing it for. With Gabe and Sienna getting engaged this week, she was thinking about the extreme circumstances that had led her and Josiah together and how she could have missed him so easily. How she could have responded so differently to his letter and the exposure of her relationship with Steven. She could be wearing this dress for someone else she wasn't meant to be with, but she wasn't. She was safe with her choice. She was sure of it. And she'd never been happier in her life.

They'd spent last weekend with her family, so after her fitting at the boutique, they decided to go to the beach for the remainder of the afternoon, and they spent most of their time before dinner in a sand dune cove sheltered from the wind and hidden from beachcombers along the thunderous surf. She felt very loved and safe with Josiah, even though their kissing had more of an intimate quality to it than they'd ever shared before. She was anxious to be at school with him in the fall when they wouldn't have to squeeze all of their spare time together into one day of the week. It made her feel weaker and more needy, and she didn't know how to stop feeling that way.

Moving his lips away from hers when she could tell it was difficult for him to do so, Josiah replaced his kissing with a long hug, and her desire for more faded as she reminded herself she and Josiah had so much more in their relationship than physical pleasure. They had that, and by the end of the year they would be able to share more than they could now, but they also had love and purity and friendship and an openness before God that she wouldn't trade for a moment that could taint all of that. It wouldn't be unforgivable or beyond God's grace, but it wouldn't be for the best either, and she didn't want that.

"Was it a mistake for us to come here?" Josiah asked. "Should we go now?"

"No," she said. "Just hold me, Josiah. I need time with you, but this is all I need."

It was getting close to dinnertime, so they only stayed for a little while longer and then went to a seafood place for clam chowder and shared a basket of Fish and Chips. She told him about how she felt while trying on her dress today, and he said he felt the same way about her being the right choice for him, and that he never doubted that. He sometimes doubted she would remain satisfied with him, but not that he wanted her in his life forever.

"Now what makes you say that?" she scolded him. "What more could I possibly want than what I have in you?"

At that same moment he spotted someone out of the corner of his eye, and he shifted his gaze to see Nick and Elissa being seated at a table along the window. He didn't think either of them had seen him, and since he didn't know they were going out or know either of them well, he didn't jump up to go say hello, but he used Nick as an example of what he meant.

"Four inches taller. Broad chest, defined biceps, dark wavy hair—a real man, not," he pointed to himself, "—this."

She laughed. "Who are you looking at," she asked, turning around in the chair.

"Nick. He just came in with Elissa."

"Oh really?" she said, turning back around without staring for too long. "That's an interesting twist. I thought he liked Michaela?"

"Both of them are news to me," he said. He didn't keep up with the latest camp romances that were brewing.

"Yes, Nick is quite the looker," she said. "Mmm, maybe I'll have to try and get his attention myself since I have such a wimpy boyfriend."

"Hey, that's wimpy fiancé."

She reached under the table and tried to tickle his knee. "Not for much longer if I keep hearing such ridiculous things come out of your mouth."

He laughed and pushed her hand away. "You're crazy, beautiful."

"I hope you're not just now figuring that out."

He waved her closer with his finger, and she leaned toward him. Their lips met and he whispered the words he meant with all of his heart. If she wanted to love him, he wasn't arguing.

"I love you."

"I love you more," she replied.

Chapter Twenty-Two

Sitting down at the table across from Nick, Elissa felt happy and amazed by how this day was going. She'd never had such a great time with a guy before, and they hadn't even been doing anything all that exciting. Just walking around Newport like they had both done before with other people, but they were doing far more than just shopping and enjoying the tourist attractions.

They'd talked easily with one another on the two-hour drive here, had lunch at Mo's when they arrived, and then walked along the Newport Bayfront, stopping at many places down one way and up the other side. They had gone to all the popular exhibits and had done a fair amount of shopping in between their other stops, mostly looking rather than buying, but she had found some things for herself, Michaela, and her dad and Gina.

She'd forgotten about getting them a wedding gift and saw a canvas painting of the ocean she thought they might like to put up in the house. She had it shipped there as the store offered to do for her so she wouldn't have to carry it around or try and pack it in her car at the end of the summer with all of her other things. Making the purchase had been a bit of a healing step for her. She had accepted her dad's remarriage fine, but losing her mother in the first place was still something she struggled with, and sending the painting made her feel like she accepted it a little more.

Nick had been by her side when she'd done it, and his presence had been similar to the rest of their time together today. She didn't feel uncomfortable at any time and felt comforted by his closeness on several occasions. Buying the painting had been one of them. Being with him made her feel different than she ever had before. She couldn't describe it.

He hadn't kissed her yet, but he had plenty of other ways of making her feel like his girlfriend instead of someone he was merely spending the day with. He held her hand often and had this way of touching the small of her back when they were entering a place and he would let her go ahead of him, or when they were looking at something together. It made her take a deep breath every time.

He opened his menu and looked at it, and she did the same. Their server came shortly, and they both ordered clam chowder and an entree, and then they were alone for only a moment before others came over to the table to say hello. She had gotten to know Rachael this summer as one of her fellow counselors, but she didn't know Josiah well. He was quiet and kept mostly to his camper guys during the week. But she liked both of them, and she was happy to see them in this surprising way.

They didn't stay long, just stopped by to say hello on their way out, and once they were gone, Nick focused his attention completely on her and asked her something seriously.

"Are you having a good day?"

"Yes," she smiled.

"What have you liked about it?"

"Everything. But mostly just being with you."

"That's good to know. I feel the same way."

She didn't understand why, but she accepted his honesty, and she chose to believe in the perfect date it had been, but when he told her something she didn't know, she felt like there was no way this could possibly be happening.

"You want to know a secret?" he asked, stirring his Coke glass with his straw.

"What?"

"This is my first date."

She stared at him, similar to the way she had on the deck this morning when he first asked her out, but she managed to reply. "What?"

"You're the first girl I've ever asked out, and as first dates go, I hope I'm not doing too badly at it."

"No, you're not," she laughed. "How can this be your first date?"

"I didn't date in high school. I was too shy around girls I thought were nice, and I either wasn't attracted to the others or I didn't like them. In college I wasn't around girls much except during class, and I was mostly socially withdrawn by that point anyway. I guess you could say I was a cynic when it came to love or anything having to do with relationships. You know those guys who walked around your high school, never looking at anybody, walking with their head down, and sitting in the back of class not saying anything?"

"Yes."

"That was me. I wasn't a partier, or a nerd, or a jock—I was nothing. Invisible—at least that's how I felt and tried to be. It wasn't until after I found Jesus and starting going to church that I began to get interested in dating, but even then I wanted to wait for someone I really wanted to ask out, not just pick whoever was available."

"So, why me?"

"I don't know," he said, smiling at her. She thought he had a great smile. "Just something about you. Working with you in the kitchen last week did something to my heart. Something I couldn't shake."

"And now, after spending most of the day with me?"

He reached across the table and took one of her hands, lifted it to his lips, and kissed her fingers. "I don't want today to be over so soon. This has been the best day of the whole summer."

She thought about how this day wouldn't have been possible if she hadn't mailed that letter to Cory this week, and she realized the urgency behind the leading in her heart. She could have decided to mail it after discovering Nick was interested in her, but there was joy in knowing she had been obedient to that Voice without knowing the reason behind it at the time; and it also made her feel like Jesus was involved in this thing between them.

She hadn't ever felt that way about the other guys she dated. It had only been about what she wanted or someone else wanted for her.

After enjoying a nice dinner together, they went down to the beach to walk for a bit, but it was cold and windy. They decided to drive back to camp, and on the way he asked her about the specifics of counseling and admitted his nervousness about tomorrow. She knew he would do fine and told him so.

He was concerned he didn't understand enough about God and the Bible to lead a bunch of high school guys in the spiritual focus of the week, but if what she'd heard from him today was any indication of his understanding of God in very real-life terms, she didn't only think he'd be a good spiritual mentor to them, but a great one.

He said several things she'd never thought about in that way before, and he had a passion for knowing God's Word she envied greatly. He reminded her of her dad in that way. Her dad had always been one to find solutions to problems or get through difficult things by saying, 'The Bible teaches us...so let's do that.' And she could see Nick being that way too.

Before they reached the camp, they stopped at a small parking area along the mountain road that led to a waterfall. There was a trail to get to the creek, and then the waterfall was a little further down. It wasn't a huge one like some she'd seen in the Northwest forests, but it had a peaceful sound and was still visible in the semi-darkness of twilight. She didn't think she had ever been here except during the day before, and being here with Nick definitely stirred up hopes he might kiss her.

He pulled her close to him when they were on the bridge. It spanned the wide section of the creek that the waterfall plunged into. She looked into his face and enjoyed the feeling of being in his arms for the first time all day.

"How are you feeling about mailing that letter to Cory this week?"

She smiled because Cory was the furthest thing from her mind at the moment. And it was obvious to her now just how shallow their relationship had been. They may have been dating for several months, talked on the phone and online a lot, and had fun times together, but beyond a physical closeness, there was none. She felt closer to Nick after one day and no kissing than she had felt with Cory—ever.

"I'm feeling very good about it."

"And how are you feeling about the possibility of you and me taking this beyond today and yet being in two different states by this time next month?"

She thought about that seriously, but she knew she would rather be with Nick and have him be in another state from her than to be with someone at a nearby school who didn't share her faith. Talking about God with Nick today, sharing personal details about how her relationship with Jesus this summer had changed, and hearing about his own transformation: she'd never been able to be that way with Cory; and she knew being away from Nick during the school year might be difficult, but not as great of a barrier as being with someone who she couldn't share that part of her heart with.

She told Nick that but then added something else. "Although to be honest, I have been considering not going back to Lifegate this year."

"Just today?"

"No, for awhile. Being closer to my dad might be for the best. I miss him."

"Would you go to school or just live at home and work?"

"I don't know. I haven't thought it through that much. I'm not sure I want to live at home, but maybe go to a school that's only one or two hours away instead of eight."

"How far is U of O from where you live?"

She smiled. "About two hours. My dad would love that."

"So would I," he said.

Another thought entered her mind, something that gave her a free feeling. She didn't want to go back to being Abby's roommate. Being away from her this summer had made a reality obvious: Abby had a very negative influence on her. She wasn't a nice person. She didn't make good choices and led others around her to do the same.

She'd been her best friend forever, but that wasn't a good thing. Elissa cared about her, but she couldn't continue to be around her right now in such a close way. Having a best friend who claimed to be a Christian but didn't act like it was as damaging as having a boyfriend who didn't acknowledge God at all. Maybe more so.

Feeling like she might cry over the huge burden she felt lifting from her weary soul, and the gratefulness she had for the way Jesus was being so faithful to her even when she hadn't always been that way with Him, she slipped her arms around Nick's neck, hugged him, and spoke her thoughts.

"I don't want to go back. I need friendships like this, not the ones I have there."

She had told him a little about Abby earlier today, so he knew why she said that, but he pointed out another truth. "Michaela will be there."

She knew that would be a major plus of going back, but she also knew she needed something more than a supportive friend like Michaela at this point in her life.

"I know," she whispered. "But you won't."

He held her close and stroked her back and made her feel like he was accepting what was happening between them without reservation. "I'd love to kiss you right now, Elissa. Would that be all right?"

She released her hold around his neck and brought her face into direct line with his. "Yes," she said, unable to hold back a smile and feeling God had planned this day just for her, gently guiding her toward it all summer long. "I'd love for you to kiss me, Nick."

His lips were sweet and gentle and tasted like cinnamon because he'd been chewing gum earlier, and even though she'd been kissed a lot by Cory and a few other guys she would have rather never kissed, Nick's had a completely different effect on her. She enjoyed it on every level, and Nick seemed to enjoy it very much also.

"I hope that was okay," he said. "I've never done this before either."

"You can do it again," she answered.

He smiled and kissed her again, and he didn't stop for a long time. When he did, darkness was surrounding them and she shivered a little from the cold. He was very warm, and the slight separation from him was noticeable, as was the disconnection she felt compared to when he was kissing her. She'd never experienced that before. Kissing had always been merely a physical act, but with Nick it was something entirely different.

She recalled something her dad had told her when she'd asked him how he knew he was meant to marry Gina. He said, 'She makes me feel how I always felt with your mother.' At the time she hadn't understood the significance of that because all the guys she'd been with had felt the same to her. They didn't all kiss her or hold her the same way, but the way they made her feel on the inside was basically the same. She hadn't realized it until now, but she didn't connect with them emotionally.

"You make me feel like a part of you," she told Nick here and now. "Like I started this day as the girl I've always been, but now you're opening up this whole new side of me I don't know."

"I know her," he whispered. "It's the girl I've seen ever since God opened my eyes. And I really, really like her."

He kissed her on the forehead and wrapped his arms around her shoulders, and she leaned into his chest, and they just stood there, holding each other. Elissa closed her eyes and listened to the sound of the waterfall and felt a mild breeze tickling her cheeks.

She wasn't sure what the rest of the summer was going to be like, or her life in general, but she knew it was never going to be the same.

Chapter Twenty-Three

When Michaela saw Nick sitting all alone on the bench beside the office at ten-thirty at night, she wondered how his day with Elissa had turned out, why he was sitting there, and where Elissa was now. Strolling up to him on the way to her room, she sat beside him and asked the first question on her mind.

"How was your day?"

He smiled adorably. "Pretty great."

"Yeah?"

"We went to the beach, and we just got back. She has something she wants to show me, so I'm waiting for her here."

"Did you kiss her?"

"Yes."

"Nicholas!"

He laughed and made no apologies. "I couldn't help myself. She's so—. I don't know. I can't describe it."

"That's great," she said. "Really. I'm very happy for you, and for Elissa. She needs this right now."

"What did you do today?"

"After I got back from town with Amber and Seth, Matt and Mandy and Adam and Lauren were waiting to see if we wanted to go down to the reservoir with them, so we all did that. Megan and Justin were already there with some others, so we were lake-bums all day. It was fun."

"Was Jake there?"

"Yes, and don't start," she laughed. "You were my best hope for meeting my dream-guy this summer, not Jake. He's too full of himself. Maybe I'll meet someone at school this year."

"Guess what?"

"What?"

"Elissa might transfer to U of O."

"Why doesn't that surprise me?"

Michaela decided to leave before Elissa came back. She didn't want to interrupt their date, and she could get the scoop on this later from Elissa. She gave Nick a brief hug and told him good-night and proceeded on her way. She didn't feel especially tired yet because she'd taken a little nap on the shore of the lake this afternoon.

Blake and Colleen were sitting on the steps of the senior staff housing area, and she stopped to say a brief hello to them. They'd gone to Crater Lake together today, she had heard from Blake this morning, and she asked them how their day had been. They both sounded like they'd had a nice time, and she wasn't surprised. They were a very solid couple that didn't get much time together during the week, so they tried to make up for it on Saturdays, and she didn't want to interrupt their last hour together either, so she told them good-night and went to her room.

She had been with others all day, and she welcomed the solitude. She spent most of the time praying. Lying on her bed and just thinking about all of the things that happened this week and whom she had promised to pray for got her started, and then she also thought of her own needs and struggles she'd either been putting out of her mind or trying to carry all by herself.

I don't know how I'm supposed to feel about my mom getting married, Jesus. I want to be happy for her, but I can't help but wonder, 'Is it right? Is she making a mistake? Can this marriage be anything better than what she had with Dad, and how am I supposed to feel about this man who will become a part of my life?' On the one hand I'm glad to be going back to school in a month where I won't have to deal with any of it for now, but another part of me is afraid for my mom and wondering if I should be there to make sure things are okay, or if I should try and talk her out of this.

As soon as she said the last part, she knew that wasn't her burden to carry. She needed to leave her mom in God's hands and let Jesus be the one to guide her in taking this step. Maybe He had brought someone who could really love her the way she needed to be loved. Maybe Tom was a wonderful person who was an answer to her mother's prayers. Or maybe he wasn't, but it wasn't her place to make that judgment.

Others came to mind then, and she prayed for them too. Some she wasn't sure why she felt the need to pray for, like Kerri, but she prayed for them anyway, asking God to be close to their hearts right now and make them very aware of His love for them. She prayed the same for herself. She needed that so much. It was so easy to lose sight of, but she couldn't afford to. She needed to believe in God's love for her every day. His constant presence and His love. If she believed in that, she could face anything.

***

Kerri was lying in bed, waiting for the nauseous feeling to pass. When it didn't, she got out of bed, went to the bathroom of the hotel room, and threw up. Just like she'd done yesterday morning.

She didn't have much to throw up, and she felt better after she did. Washing her face with one of the white washcloths and patting it dry with a fresh hand towel, she felt the color returning to her cheeks and took a drink of water. Going back to bed, she saw Kevin was still asleep and knew he hadn't heard her being sick, just like he hadn't yesterday. She pulled the blankets up to her chest. She felt better and knew she could fall back to sleep instantly, but she took a moment to accept an obvious reality.

She was pregnant. She'd known it before now, but she had been in denial. For the last two weeks she'd been telling herself to relax and not panic. She was late because of the stress of the wedding, or because of the changes in her schedule since being on her honeymoon, or because of going on a cruise. Deep down she knew her reasons were ridiculous. If one of her friends gave her those kinds of excuses for their period being late, she would laugh at them—at least on the inside. And she'd be telling them, 'Face it, sister. You're pregnant.'

But she hadn't been able to face it yet. She had put off buying a pregnancy test until she was a full two weeks late, and then when she'd seen the positive result last Saturday morning, she still tried to deny it. She hadn't said anything to Kevin. She hadn't even uttered the possibility to God—and she talked to Him about everything. But not this. This couldn't be happening to her. How could He let this happen to her?

She let the tears fall for the first time, but they were quiet tears so she wouldn't wake Kevin. Having children with him was something she wanted. Just not this soon. Her plan had been to wait at least five years. When she was finished with school. When she was twenty-five, not nineteen. What had she done to deserve this? She didn't understand.

It was early, so she fell back asleep. She had a dream where she had the baby and was holding it in her arms. They were at her baby shower, and everybody was so happy. Everyone but her.

Kevin woke her by snuggling into her back. He wasn't fully awake, and lying there silently, she waited to see if he would go back to sleep. They'd been having such a wonderful honeymoon together. She knew this baby had been conceived in so much love, like she had always prayed would be the case for her children. But now the joy was overshadowed with it not seeming like the right time.

She wished she was at home so she could talk to her mom. But she wasn't, and she didn't think she wanted to tell her over the phone. They were going to be there later next week, but she didn't know if she could hide this from Kevin for much longer. Physically speaking she could probably get away with passing her morning sickness off as the flu, but in her heart she knew she needed to tell him. She had already put it off too long.

Feeling the security of his arms around her, she fully accepted the fact he was her husband. She thought she had done so on her wedding day, but she hadn't. So far she'd been playing Bride Barbie. She was married and with her husband on their honeymoon like she'd always dreamed about. But this was more than that. This was her life. This was their life together. This was reality, not something to 'play' and then move on to something else.

But she knew it wasn't a mistake. She hadn't chosen hastily. God had led her into this relationship, and it had been perfect from the beginning. Sometimes scary, sometimes confusing, sometimes challenging, but always right. She couldn't doubt that now. It would cripple her to stop believing in their love.

She fell asleep again, and neither of them stirred until nine o'clock. This time she woke up feeling hungry and only slightly nauseous, so she didn't argue when Kevin suggested going down to get something from the informal breakfast room. Kevin had cereal, and she had yogurt, part of a bagel, and hot tea. The tea seemed to make her feel better, and she took a second cup back to the room.

They were supposed to be meeting the others in the hotel lobby at eleven. A car would pick them up out front and take them to the train station where they would take a two-day trip through the remote Alaskan landscape. They had taken several train rides during their time here in Alaska, and she enjoyed traveling in that way and seeing all the varied places and beauty that was more spectacular and vast than she'd ever imagined.

But she didn't think she was up for it today.

Kevin usually let her shower first since it took her longer to get ready, but she decided to tell him. She didn't want to take a shower or go anywhere. Just staying in her pajamas and lying in bed all day sounded really good.

He sat on the bed to remove his shoes, and she sat beside him. He looked at her like this wasn't their routine, and she was reminded of how quickly they had fallen into one. Even with traveling from city to city and staying in various hotels, riding on trains, and on a cruise ship, they still had formed a rhythm of everyday life together.

"I have something to tell you," she said. "Something that may change our plans for today."

"What?" he asked.

"Before I tell you, will you kiss me and tell me you love me?"

He appeared a little confused by her request, but he did so. Kissing her briefly at first but then sensing her need for more and giving it to her. She kissed him back and got lost in his touch like always.

"I love you, Kerri," he said. "You're my wife, and I love you."

"I love you too," she said, saying it more for herself than him. She didn't know why this was happening right now, but she knew it was happening to them together. She was pregnant, but it wasn't just her baby, it was theirs.

She looked him in the eye. She didn't have any idea how he was going to react. Would he even know what she meant? Would he be upset, like when he knew Jenna was getting married and didn't want that kind of change? Thinking about the possibility of him not being supportive, or being aloof, made her feel like she couldn't say it, so she said it quickly before she could change her mind.

"I'm pregnant, Kevin. We're going to have a baby."

He stared at her for a moment and then smiled. "We are?"

"Yes."

"Wow!" he said. "That's exciting."

She smiled.

"When?"

"Sometime next year. Around April, I think."

"That's awhile," he said.

"It takes awhile, but it's already gotten started," she said, looking down at her flat tummy and placing her hand on her lower abdomen. When she looked up at him, he was just staring at her.

"Why are you sad?" he asked.

She didn't try to deny it. "I wasn't planning on us having a baby this soon. I wanted to finish school first and have a few years of it just being you and me, but I guess God has other plans. He's giving us a baby now—next year, I mean."

Kevin didn't seem to know what to say.

"It's okay," she said, giving him a little smile and not wanting to alarm him too much. "I'm not sad really, just surprised. You know how you get things set in your mind a certain way and it's hard to accept when that changes?"

"Yes."

"This is like that for me," she said, suddenly realizing she couldn't be talking to the more perfect person. If anyone would understand the difficulty of accepting a huge change from her original mindset, it would be Kevin. And she also felt like she understood Kevin's heart and mind better. This was what he had to deal with all the time in everyday life.

"Would it be all right if we didn't go on the train today?" she asked. "I've been feeling sick the last couple of days. Nothing is wrong. That's normal for a woman who is pregnant, but a train ride might make me feel worse. I'd like to stay here and rest."

"We can stay," he said without any hesitation, which she knew was a big deal for him. He had their schedule for the week memorized down to the smallest detail, but he was willing to change all that for her, just because she said she needed it.

"Thank you."

She put her arms around his neck, and he held her. "I'll help when the baby comes," he said. "I'll help you."

"I know you will."

"I-I-I'll take care of it while you're at school. I-I'll be done by then, and you can k-keep go-going."

She had a mental picture of going into labor one Friday afternoon and being back in class on Monday, and she laughed.

"Why is that funny?" he asked.

"It's not," she said, sitting back and taking his words seriously. "It's very sweet of you to say, and I know you're going to be a great daddy. I'm just laughing at me. I shouldn't be so surprised by this. God is always messing with my plans."

"And you like that?" he asked, not appearing to understand how that could be good, and she understood why. Most of the time Kevin's mind seemed to track with God's plans just fine. He would suggest something that seemed totally crazy to her but would be right on with what she really needed—like ending up on a date with him, and going to New York with him over Christmas, and marrying him last month.

But her own plans were mostly that—her own plans. Without God stepping in and changing course on her, she would be so far off the track by now. It would be like ending up in the Alaskan Wilderness in wintertime when she was supposed to be in sunny Florida.

"Yes, I like that," she said. "Last summer at this time I had no idea I'd be married by now, or sitting here having this conversation with you, but now that I am, I can't imagine being anyplace else. And if I followed Him and ended up with you, I know I just need to keep following. My plans are my plans, but His plans are perfect."

Chapter Twenty-Four

Seeing Elissa getting ready on Sunday morning in front of the bathroom mirror while she was doing the same, Lauren couldn't help but notice the near constant smile on Elissa's face. She hadn't gotten to know Elissa super-well this summer. Partly because they were both counseling and it was difficult to find time to talk to each other on a personal level, and partly because they had formed different circles of friends this summer and rarely spent any time together on the weekends either.

Lauren hadn't been feeling uncomfortable with having Elissa here. She kept to herself a lot, and even though Lauren had seen her acting in negative ways with Abby on campus this year, she acted different here. It had been easy for Lauren to see that Elissa was actually very quiet and self-conscious on her own.

"Did you have a good Saturday?" Lauren asked. They were the only two out by the sinks at the moment, and it seemed like a good thing to ask.

Elissa smiled before she answered. "Yes."

"What did you do?"

Elissa took a deep breath and let it out before responding in a calm yet happy voice. "I went to the beach with Nick."

Lauren knew of Nick, but she didn't know him as anything besides one of the older guys on crew staff. "Oh," she said, not having any reason to object to the news. She thought she remembered Elissa saying something about having a boyfriend she was away from this summer, but she didn't know anything about their relationship or that it had apparently ended at some point.

"I didn't know the two of you were going out."

"We weren't," Elissa laughed. "Not until yesterday."

"Oh?" Lauren said, feeling more intrigued now. "And it went well?"

There was that deep breath and smile again. "Yes, it was amazing. I've never had a date like that."

Lauren smiled, recalling how she'd felt the same way about Adam. "I know what that's like. I'm happy for you."

"Thanks. I just hope it was real, you know?"

She knew that feeling too. "Has he dated other girls here this summer?"

"No. And he hasn't dated before this summer either."

That surprised Lauren because Nick was good-looking and very social from what she'd observed this summer. "Not at all?"

"No. Before he knew God, he was very introverted and mostly a loner—the kind who don't talk to anybody and just exist from one day to the next. It's hard to imagine with the way he is now, huh? But that's what he says."

"What did you like about spending the day with him?"

"Everything. I could just be me and that's who he likes."

"I know that feeling," Lauren said.

Elissa seemed thoughtful for a moment. "And you know? I think this is the first time in my life I've ever felt that way other than with my family. Even with Abby, my best friend since forever: I was always trying to be someone else with her."

"Who were you trying to be?"

"Like her, I guess. But I don't know why. She's been mostly a negative influence on me. She doesn't treat other people well, and she doesn't do the right things and make good choices."

Lauren didn't say anything about what she knew on that subject, but she did say something else she knew could be true. "Maybe it's time to have a new best friend."

Elissa's happy smile returned. "Yes, I think so too."

When Lauren saw Adam twenty minutes later, she gave him an extra long hug, remembering how he was absolutely her best friend, and she didn't want to take that for granted. They'd been together for almost a year, and sometimes it was easy to forget how close they really were. They weren't married or engaged yet, but she believed that was in their future.

"I'll miss you this week," she said to explain her clinginess.

"We have a few hours yet."

"I know, but I wish we had another full day."

"Me too, Angel. Only three more weeks."

She didn't respond. Three weeks seemed like a long time right now, and all the things she'd been telling herself all summer about being grateful she and Adam were here together instead of spending the summer in different locations, and being happy the guy she was dating was following Jesus like she was, and knowing they would be seeing each other every day once they were back at school: none of that meant anything right now.

"I love you, Lauren," he said most tenderly.

"I love you too, Adam. So much, it hurts sometimes."

"Tell you what," he said.

"What?"

"Next Saturday, and the one after that: you and me, Silver Falls, all day."

"Okay," she said, feeling a little better.

"And," he added. "Every morning this week: you and me on our bench at the lake?"

She released him slightly and looked into his eyes. "Yeah?"

"I'll meet you at six-thirty."

"In the morning?"

"Yes. If I can do the counselor meeting at seven, I can meet you at six-thirty. You've been too easy on me about that."

"I've been okay up until now."

"I'll be there, Angel. I promise."

***

Adam had the best week of the summer, and by Thursday he was kicking himself for not making a habit of meeting Lauren every morning before now. He'd thought about it the first week, but he didn't think he could do it. He didn't want to start something he couldn't follow through with, but now he knew that had been a mistake. He'd gotten so used to seeing Lauren every day at school that he had forgotten how difficult it could be to be away from her.

The last few weeks he'd been feeling a little down: going through the motions of counseling and having good weeks in general, and yet feeling like something was missing. But after this week, he knew what it was. Undeniably it had been time with Lauren. Those extra thirty minutes made all the difference.

After sharing about how their week was going and reading some verses in Psalms like they'd been doing all summer, but usually during their break in the afternoon, he asked her something he had been thinking about last night. He'd had a difficult time going to sleep because he had a lot on his mind, and he'd thought about something he knew he should probably ask her, rather than just assume.

"How are you feeling about going back to school?"

"I can't wait," she said, but he knew she wasn't thinking about school, just about being able to see him every day on a more unlimited basis.

"I mean about school, school," he clarified. "Are you feeling up for it, or dreading it?"

"Mostly dreading it," she laughed. "Although, I was talking to Amber one day last week, and she's going to be taking classes this year outside the general sophomore core, like Bible classes and ministry-focused ones—more for herself instead of to meet standardized requirements—and I was thinking of doing the same thing. Maybe even choosing the same ones she does. What do you think of that?"

"Whatever you want to do. I'll just be happy you're there, but I want you to be happy about being there too."

"I'll be okay. This summer has reminded me of how much joy I can have by having time with you."

"This week has reminded me of that." He reached for her hand and held it loosely for a moment. "On Sunday I made this commitment for you, but today I'm promising another two weeks for me. I need you, Lauren. More than I realize sometimes."

She seemed thoughtful for a moment. "Can I ask you something?"

"Anything."

"Have you ever thought about breaking up with me?"

He smiled. "No. Never."

"Really?"

"Yes. Why? Have you thought about breaking up with me?"

"No. I just have a difficult time believing this is real, you know? Like, 'The guy I'm dating actually loves me, and it's Adam.' It just seems crazy to me."

"It's not crazy," he said, pulling her close to him and holding her in his arms. "You're everything I need, Lauren. And you're everything I want. And I love you because you are incredibly easy to love."

"You're easy to love too. Thanks for loving me for exactly who I am."

Adam made a point of talking to Seth that afternoon. He had a question to ask him about knowing when was the right time to get married. He knew he wanted to marry Lauren, but the question was, when? Next summer? After he graduated? He could see advantages and disadvantages to each. He loved the thought of getting married, but it also scared him. He used to think he wouldn't feel that way when he got older, but with his twentieth birthday coming up in another two months, he wasn't sure age had anything to do with it.

***

Kerri and Kevin arrived in Portland late Thursday evening, and it hadn't been a great day. She felt very sick this morning, and it hadn't gone away. She'd thrown up in the bathroom on the plane twice and again in the airport after they landed.

Her mom and dad had come to meet them, and they knew she wasn't feeling well, but they didn't know why. She had wanted to wait and tell them in person, but since she was rarely sick like this, she wondered if they'd already figured it out.

They didn't say anything and got her home as quickly as possible. She felt better than she had all day, and she didn't think she could have any more to throw up, but by the time they got to the house, she did so once again in the downstairs bathroom.

She and Kevin were going to be sleeping in her bedroom while they were here, and once her mom had helped her get semi-undressed and under the covers, she decided to tell her. Kevin had gone down to the kitchen to get something to eat for himself. It was well past dinnertime, and he hadn't eaten anything except in-flight snacks since lunch.

Her mom felt her forehead and was about to go get the thermometer, but she stopped her. "I'm not sick, Mom." She paused and then whispered it. "I'm pregnant."

She started crying. She had slowly accepted this as being a good thing and a part of God's plan for them, but she still felt scared and didn't fully understand. And she didn't feel well right now. She hated being sick and knew this wasn't going to go away after a few days. She could be feeling like this for several more weeks or even months.

Her mom held her gently like she would expect, and she didn't say anything until her tears subsided. "You know the only time I cried about being pregnant?"

"When?"

"When I already had three children and I found out I was having twins."

Kerri laughed. That would have been with her and Seth. She'd heard her parents say before they had been unplanned. They were stopping with three, and then when Micah had barely turned one, they found out they were having another: and not just one, but two.

"Does Kevin know?" her mom asked.

"Yes. I told him—after I finally accepted the reality for myself."

"How did he take it?"

Kerri smiled and felt better just thinking about it. "He's excited." She paused and then added. "He's really my husband, isn't he?"

"Yes, honey. He is."

"I'm not sure that hit me until last week."

"And how has it been, having him as your husband?"

"Great. Just like I knew it would be."

Her dad came into the room and sat behind her mom on the edge of the bed. Reaching out to take her other hand, he asked if she was feeling any better.

"A little," she said, wondering if the stress of coming home today had contributed to being more sick than usual. She knew she'd been feeling nervous about telling her family the news. Not that she had anything to be ashamed of, but they all knew she had her plan, and this was not part of it.

"I'm pregnant, Daddy."

"I know. Kevin told me."

She smiled. "He wasn't supposed to."

"I asked him. I had a feeling. I am a doctor, you know."

"I know! What's with those faulty pills my doctor gave me? They didn't work!"

"Sorry," he said, like he'd had to tell his own patients the same thing. "Sometimes they don't."

She let out a frustrated growl, but he laughed.

"It'll be all right, sweetheart. You always rise to the challenge."

Talking with her parents made her feel better, and when Kevin came up and they left to let her rest, his company at the end of this long day was what she needed most. He asked if he could get into bed.

"Yes, I need you, Kevin. I'm sorry if I scared you earlier. If I had known I was going to be that sick, I would have waited a day or two to have us fly home."

He changed into his pajamas and got underneath the blankets, snuggling up next to her before he said anything.

"I love you, Kerri. I'm sorry you're sick."

"I know you are." She turned her head and gave him a kiss. "I'm sorry I got sick on the plane. I know that scared you."

He didn't deny it, and she suddenly realized what a mixed-up, crazy day this must have been for him, but he wasn't doing too badly with it. "Are you sure you want to be married to me, Kevin? I know all of this is messing with your world. I'm not a perfect pizza."

"You're not a pizza."

"No? What am I?"

"You're a girl."

"I'm not a perfect one of those either."

He didn't say anything else, and she knew he probably needed quiet time with her, so she remained silent. She stopped thinking about the baby and her anxiety related to that and recalled the last six weeks she'd spent with him, traveling from here to San Francisco, then to Alaska on a cruise ship, and all around an unfamiliar but beautiful place, staying in fancy hotels with nice restaurants, and riding in ferry boats and trains. It had all been magnificent: far beyond any honeymoon she'd ever imagined.

And yet the thing she enjoyed the most was the same thing they were doing now. Just being together. No matter the city or hotel or daily itinerary, Kevin was still Kevin, the love of her life, and she was still Kerri, whom he loved for whatever crazy reason.

"Are you still awake?" she whispered.

"Yes."

"I need to go to the bathroom and brush my teeth. But I'll be right back, okay?"

"Okay. Are you sick again?"

"No, I don't think so. I feel better now."

She left the room and went into the hall bath. When she returned, she changed out of the shirt she'd been wearing, that probably smelled awful, and put on one of her prettier nightgowns made of silky fabric that only hung partway down her thighs. It had spaghetti straps and had been one she remembered Kevin having a particular liking for.

He couldn't see her in the dark room, but when she got into bed, he could feel she'd changed into something he liked, and he didn't hesitate to comment on it.

"You feel nice."

"I thought you might need a little "nice" at the end of this day."

She kissed him, initiating the intimate time with the intention of giving him something to end this day on a good note, but she found she needed it too. She needed the reminder of his love. She needed the security of his embrace. And she needed to remember that none of this was a mistake.

Before Kevin drifted off to sleep, he said something he hadn't said to her until after they'd gotten married, but he'd said it often since, and she needed to hear it tonight.

"I love you, Kerri. For ever and ever."

"For ever and ever," she echoed.

Chapter Twenty-Five

It felt good to get out of the house. Sienna felt like yesterday was a million miles away. Nothing major had happened, but it had been one of those days when being a mother seemed overwhelming and too hard for her to handle at nineteen.

Gabe had worked later than usual because two of the evening delivery drivers had called in sick, and he'd had to fill in until the Friday night dinner-rush died down enough for him to get out of there. He'd caught her in a bad moment when he arrived at the house, and her frustrations weren't about him or even the fact he was later than she was expecting, but she'd unloaded on him anyway.

Fortunately Gabe had been in an understanding and "let me help however I can" mood, or she may have lost him and been kissing her wedding plans good-bye, instead of being on a mission to accomplish as much as possible for the day coming up in just three more weeks.

She picked up her friend Elizabeth first, and they went to lunch together. Lizzy was very interested in hearing about what the last two weeks had been like. She'd been out of town because her family had gone to southern California on a two-week vacation, and they'd left the day after Gabe had proposed to her, so their farewell had been like, 'Have a good time on your trip, and oh, by the way, I'm getting married.'

Lizzy had been her surprise best friend through all of this. They'd known each other for a long time but hadn't been close friends. Mostly because she had held Lizzy at arm's length while she tried to gain approval from girls in other crowds at school. But they attended the same church, and other than Gabe, Lizzy had been the first person she had told about being pregnant.

Lizzy had been a supportive friend through all of it. She had been there at the hospital on the night Brittany was born. Lizzy had been the one to help her turn it all over to God instead of trying to put the pieces back together herself. She had told her repeatedly that coercing Gabe into marrying her wasn't the right solution, and that she needed to admit her need for a Savior in this as much as she needed Him for security in her eternal destiny.

"Is this for real?" Lizzy asked her point-blank after they had both ordered their food. "Is he for real, Sienna? Are you sure?"

Sienna knew her friend was just expressing her concern. She'd been through so much with her already. But Sienna also knew this is exactly what Lizzy had been praying for—and had convinced her to pray for too.

"It's for real," she said. "Everything I was hoping for in my heart is happening, and on the one hand I'm thinking, 'This is too good to be true,' but on the other

I know this is the miracle we asked God for, and He did it for me, Lizzy. Jesus did it."

Lizzy smiled and had tears in her eyes too. "I guess I shouldn't be amazed, but I am."

"I know. Me too. And you know what's most amazing?"

"What?"

"All this time I've been praying that Gabe would start loving me, but he actually already did. It's like God knew we needed each other before we did, and He put that love into our hearts even before we would be able to handle it properly. He knew we were going to mess up but would be all right in the end, so He allowed it."

"I'm very happy for you, Sienna. I've never seen you with so much peace."

"Thank you for never letting me give up hope. So many times I thought, 'Lizzy doesn't understand how impossible this is. She's not living in reality. God blesses people like her, but not me.' But you were right all along."

When she returned to the house after her full afternoon, she told Gabe about her day and everything she had accomplished. He seemed excited about the wedding, and she didn't feel like he was faking anything, but she couldn't help but wonder if his optimistic view of getting married would last. Gabe was a spontaneous person. What if this seemed like a good idea to him now, but after they were married, he changed his mind?

She decided to ask him during Brittany's evening naptime. Her mom and dad had gone out, so they couldn't go for a walk, but she wanted to talk like they often did during that time. She knew she wanted to marry him, but she wanted to make sure he knew he wanted it too.

"I'm sure, Sienna," he said without hesitation. "I know this is the right thing for us, and I know it can work. I know we're going to be fine."

"How do you know?"

He leaned across her and reached for her copy of *The Message* on the end table beside the couch. Opening the pages, he searched for something, and she waited for him to find what he was looking for.

"I read this the night before I proposed to you," he said, taking a moment to explain before he read anything. "At the time I was wondering if I could really make that kind of commitment to you, but this chased away the doubt."

He began reading from the book of Galatians, and she just listened. At times he read continuously, and other times he seemed to search for the phrases that applied specifically to them.

> *"It is obvious what kind of life develops out of trying to get your own way all the time: repetitive, loveless, cheap sex; a stinking accumulation of mental and emotional garbage; frenzied and joyless grabs for happiness...all consuming but never-satisfied wants...divided homes and divided lives...I could go on. But what happens when we live God's way? He brings gifts into our lives, much the same way that fruit appears in an orchard—things like affection for others, exuberance about life, serenity. We develop a*

willingness to stick with things, a sense of compassion in the heart...We find ourselves involved in loyal commitments, not needing to force our way in life...Since this is the kind of life we have chosen, the life of the Spirit, let us make sure that we do not just hold it as an idea in our heads or a sentiment in our hearts, but work out its implications in every detail of our lives."

He stopped reading and looked at her. She felt emotional and could tell he was once again moved by the words.

"I finally understand, Sienna. For so long I saw God as someone I had to try and please, and I lived my life seeing how much I could get away with. And then I got you pregnant, but I thought I could walk away because it wasn't my fault.

"But then I came here, and I saw her, and I saw you again, and I realized—God is trying to bless me! I messed up. I did things the wrong way, and yet still—Here you are, and here's Brittany. What's going to happen when I actually follow God's plan? If He can bless me this much in His mercy, how much more will I be blessed when I make the right choices?"

She smiled, and peace entered her heart. This wasn't just Gabe stepping back into her life. It was Gabe following God and understanding His love, something that had transformed her heart six months ago and she continued to depend on daily.

"This is the life I want to choose for us, Sienna. And I know it will be good because God is leading us, and because I love you. I really do, Sienna. Please believe that."

She gave him a hug and held him close, not just in her arms, but in her heart. "I believe it."

***

Mariah couldn't believe the summer was almost over. Only two days of the second high school camp remained, and there was only one more week to go after this. By this time next week she would be starting to pack her things in preparation for leaving her summer home.

Walking up to the lake in the early morning sunshine that promised another warm August day, she was looking forward to seeing Warner like she had been every day this summer, and especially these last few weeks when he'd been meeting her this early. She had expected him to oversleep or not show up a time or two, but he never had, and today she was the one running late.

"Rough morning?" he asked when she met him on "their bench" overlooking the water.

"One of the showers wasn't working, so I had to wait for Elissa to finish."

He smiled, and she laughed. Warner had been the one to encourage Nick to meet with Elissa in the mornings now too, and that was not like him to do. He used to complain about guys who tried to keep him on-track spiritually or give him any relationship advice, but now he was one of them.

Last week when he'd been counseling for the first time all summer, he had discovered Jake had a thing for Michaela, and he'd been coaching him for the last two weeks on how to go about getting her the right way instead of all his lame attempts so far. And apparently something had worked because Jake had gotten her to agree to a date with him this Saturday.

"I can't believe this week is almost over," she said. "It's going by really fast for me. You too, or is it just my active girls that are making it feel that way?"

"It's going by fast. I'll be glad to get back to crew next week and slow the pace down a little before the summer ends. I'm usually ready to go home by last week, but not this year."

She smiled and felt sad at the same time. Saying good-bye to him next weekend was going to be really hard, although they had talked about spending time together before school started in September, but they hadn't decided on anything for sure.

He seemed to read her thoughts. "You know that isn't going to be the end for us, right?"

She leaned against him, and he put his arm around her. "Yes. I know."

He pulled her closer, and she had to turn her body to keep him from crushing her. Giving in to what she really wanted in that moment, she put her arms around his neck and let him hold her close, laying her head on his shoulder and breathing in his clean, soapy smell.

Normally they were much more "spiritual" about this time together, but once she was in his arms, she didn't want to end it too soon, and he wasn't in any hurry either.

"I love it when you need me, Mariah."

She smiled and wasn't ashamed to admit it.

"I need you too. Thanks for talking me into counseling. I've needed these two weeks. It's reminded me of how far I've come since my own high school days."

She smiled but didn't say it.

"Okay, since last summer."

She released him and laughed.

He smiled at her and gave her a little kiss on the cheek. "And I blame you entirely."

They went on with their normal Bible-reading then, and she let Warner share about how the words spoke to him before sharing her own thoughts. She'd found he usually shared more if she let him go first, and she loved hearing him talk about God in real-life terms. It was a new thing for him, and she liked to see him discovering things she was already familiar with and those she hadn't thought about before. He could come at things from a unique perspective because of the longer road he'd taken to begin a more personal, everyday relationship with God like she'd been experiencing for several years now.

But even with as close to Jesus as she felt, and the way she'd been praying for dealing with the summer coming to an end, she wasn't sure she was going to make it this time. In her heart she knew Jesus would give her exactly what she needed, when she needed it, like He'd done so many times in the past.

But in her head she was thinking, 'I can't handle it. It's going to be too hard to be away from him after this. And who knows when that's going to end? I could be living away from him nine months out of the year for the next five years or more! I've had a lot of patience in this, but I don't know how much more I can take.'

They were walking toward where their counselor meeting would begin in five minutes when he said something she never would have expected him to say, or had even thought about. She liked going to a state university located in her hometown so she could live at home and commute, and she'd never considered going "away" to college. Not seriously anyway. She knew she would like to live closer to Warner now that they were together and go to the same school he did, but moving to Portland wasn't something she could picture herself doing. She wasn't that adventurous.

"What would you think about both of us transferring to Lifegate in January?"

She looked at him, and he appeared serious. She'd heard a lot of good things about the school, and she knew several people here that would be there, including Michaela and Lauren who had become her two best friends this summer besides Warner.

"Are you thinking about it?"

"Yes. Adam's been trying to talk me into it, and I've told him no because they don't have a Marine Biology program, but then I found out from Blake there's a state university there in the same town. I could go to Lifegate for at least two semesters and then transfer to Humboldt to finish up my degree—If you like it there and want to stay. Or we could move back up here. But I think a year there would do me good."

She wasn't opposed to going and knew she would definitely prefer that over them living at opposite ends of the state for another three years. But she felt too shocked to speak.

"If you don't want to, I am thinking of at least transferring to U of O after this term, but I thought I'd throw that out there and see what you think. We can pray about it more. It's just an idea."

She smiled and found her voice before he talked himself out of this. "It's a good idea. I'd really like that if we can make it work."

He didn't comment immediately, and they walked the remaining distance toward the building in silence, but he stopped her before they went inside.

"I'd like it too, Mariah. Even being away from you for three months is going to be very difficult."

"Four," she corrected. "It's four months until Winter Break."

He smiled and pulled her close to him. His smile confused her until he spoke.

"Three, Mariah. I'm not going to be away from you until I absolutely have to, and that's not for another six weeks."

Chapter Twenty-Six

"What are your plans for this afternoon?"

Amber turned to look at her husband, and she smiled. They were in the middle of eating lunch with the rest of the crew staff and were surrounded by a lot of talking and laughter from the rowdy bunch. The staff always seemed to be more crazy on Fridays in anticipation of their day off.

But Seth's tone wasn't casual, like he was wondering what was on her schedule today. He had something specific in mind, and she'd been wondering if he might.

"I don't know," she replied in an equally suggestive tone. "What are you doing?"

"Taking my girl on a canoe ride, if she wants one."

It wasn't the exact date of their first canoe ride together three years ago, but it was the same Friday of the second week of high school camp, and she was definitely in the mood for a trip down memory lane and extra time with Seth. They had been focused on their leadership responsibilities most of the summer, but they had talked about taking more time for themselves during these last two weeks, and she had the feeling Seth had more than just a canoe ride in mind for this afternoon.

"I'd love one," she said, giving him a little kiss right there at the table. Earlier in the summer she'd felt strange showing him any kind of affection in front of their crew members, since that wasn't allowed for unmarried couples on staff, but lately she had felt more free to do so. She wanted the girls under her to see that waiting for the right guy and marrying him was a special thing. She wanted them to wish for a guy like Seth and a marriage like theirs.

They had things to do before they could have some free time, but once their duties had been completed and their crew staff was all where they needed to be for the afternoon, they walked to the waterfront together, holding hands and seeing the camp alive with activity on this final afternoon of the week. It reminded Amber of her final Friday as a camper when she'd hobbled up to the lake with her injured leg to meet Seth and thank him for rescuing her the night before.

She had sat there on the beach, waiting for him to arrive, and when he did, it all turned out much differently than she'd ever imagined. Going on a canoe ride with him had never entered her thought-process until he invited her to do so.

Once they were out on the water today, she enjoyed the peacefulness of the setting around them and the peaceful feeling she had in her heart of how their relationship had slowly unfolded over the last three years. They were married now, and some days she couldn't believe it, but not being married to him by this point—she couldn't imagine that. Their love was a forever kind of love, and marrying Seth hadn't been a huge leap, more like the next stepping stone on a pleasant and beautiful journey.

"How are you different today than you were three years ago?" Seth asked her. "Besides being married to me instead of barely knowing me."

She thought about that. In some ways she didn't feel any different. She was still Amber Kristine Wilson in terms of her personality and family and past experiences. She still felt very insecure at times. Sure she was a three-year veteran staff member now, married to one of the most admired guys here, senior counselor of the girls crew staff, and everyone knew her, but who was she to be any of that? She often felt more like a high school camper than a married college student in a leadership position.

But in other ways her life was very different from how it had been back then. She'd learned to see her value in the eyes of others. She'd grown to understand the importance of living her life in a pure and right way and seen how that affected her life and those around her. She'd learned the value of true friendship, both giving and receiving it. She'd fallen in love with an incredibly special guy who had changed her in so many ways, she couldn't even begin to think what her life would be like now without him. But she knew what had changed the most in the last three years, and she said it.

"I've fallen completely in love with Jesus, and I know He is completely in love with me."

Seth smiled like he knew she was going to say that. And she knew he was on that same kind of journey with her. Three years ago they were both in a place of knowing Jesus and doing their best to follow Him. But their understanding of Him had been very limited. They both had a childlike faith, and they still had that; but they'd learned what to do with it in an adult world.

They had learned the meaning of His grace. They'd grown to understand His heart. They'd seen the reality of His desire and ability to lead them as His beloved children: in their everyday lives as teenagers, in their relationship with one another, in the paths He had for their future—some of which they were already living, and more that were still to come.

She had fallen in love with Jesus. Everything about Him was good and right and made sense eventually, even if there were clouds along the way. He was faithful. He loved her. All He wanted was her belief and trust. To surrender everything to Him so He could make it all beautiful and amazing and beyond her wildest imagination.

It wasn't always easy. Some days she felt like she couldn't face the next. Sometimes she got swallowed up in fear and doubt. Sometimes her peace and joy was clouded by difficult and confusing circumstances. Often she felt inadequate and like she was completely missing the mark of what it meant to be a follower of Jesus.

But the truth always met her somewhere along the path. *'Be still and know that I am God, Amber. I love you for who you are, not for what you do for Me. Just remain in Me, and I will do it! Nothing is impossible. Love Me, Amber. Love Me with everything you have to give, and I will prove My love for you over and over again. Just trust Me. Just believe. I'm right here, always. I will bless you through this. I am your God.'*

Seth said some of those things in explaining how he had changed during the last three years. He'd known a lot of it before, but more so in an intellectual sense. He had grown up learning about Him being that kind of God. But it had been in the last three years he'd come to believe it in his heart through personal experience, not just as truth written in a book. And she could say the same for herself.

Once they were on shore again, he retook her hand and led her back to the crew housing area. They were living in a small room above the large meeting area known as the staff lounge. The building was also used as a retreat center in the fall, winter, and spring and it was very nice and spacious, but their little room was smaller than an average-sized hotel room. Their bed took up most of the open space, along with a small chair in the corner and a nightstand for a lamp. It had a small bathroom, but it wasn't big enough for both of them to be in there at the same time unless one of them was in the shower.

But their room had made for many cozy nights together, and a few afternoons when they could sneak away without anyone noticing their absence from camp activity. Amber knew God had proven His faithfulness to her in many ways over the last three years, but none more so than in this. She and Seth had waited for God's best in their relationship. Spiritually, emotionally, and physically it had always been what it should be. They'd taken the necessary steps to follow Him in that. They had talked about it. They'd prayed. They had been obedient even when it was difficult to make the right choices. Such a simple formula: wait until marriage. And they'd done that. And this was their reward.

An afternoon of passion that held no shame or regret. Love in its purest and most unhindered form. Tickling and laughter and intimate contact there was no substitute for. Just them being together and loving each other in a tangible, pleasure-filled way. Completely private and yet completely acceptable. Right in God's eyes and a healthy, vital part of their relationship now.

And she was also convinced their reward wasn't just a physical one. It was everything. Their solid, consistent friendship and love. Serving together in a vibrant ministry of leading others into a love relationship with Jesus. Everyday joy, and peace for the future. The hope to overcome no matter what life threw at them. The blessings ahead in a lifetime of loving God and each other. Of living-loved in His truth and His faithfulness.

The following day they went to Portland. Kevin and Kerri were back from their extended honeymoon, and they were looking forward to seeing them. Kerri and Kevin would be in Portland all week, and next weekend too for Matt and Mandy's wedding, but she and Seth probably wouldn't have much time with them until they were all back in California, and even then their time with Kerri and Kevin would be limited because they would be living in town instead of on campus.

Amber was expecting a mostly relaxed time with his family in the afternoon before they went out to her parents' house for dinner. Her previous summers at camp had been very good, but she'd always missed her family a lot. This summer she didn't feel like she missed them quite so much. Even if it was just the two of them, Seth had become her family as much as her own had ever been, and while she knew it would be good to see them, she didn't feel that urgency like she often had in the past.

But being with Seth's family turned out to be more eventful and exciting than she was expecting. Kerri was still Kerri, and yet there was something different about her that Amber sensed as soon as she greeted them at the front door. She appeared to have been anxiously waiting for their arrival. Kerri and Seth had always been close, and this was the most time apart they'd ever had in their nineteen years as brother and sister, but she seemed a little too happy and emotional about seeing him again just because of that factor.

Kevin was there too, and Amber gave both of them a hug, but then Kerri spoke as if she was bursting at the seams to do so.

"Guess what?"

"What?" Seth asked, seeming to know Kerri was acting a little different too.

Kerri snuggled into Kevin's side and then spoke the words. "We're going to have a baby."

"No way," Seth said.

"Yes way!" Kerri replied, beaming with her classic smile and moisture in her large brown eyes. "Can you believe it?"

"No," Seth laughed. "Can you?"

Kerri gave Kevin a light kiss and then stepped back into Seth's awaiting arms, and Amber felt dazed at the news, and her own tears formed for her sister-in-law. Kerri clung to Seth like Amber had never seen her do before, and it was a very tender moment with her brother she obviously needed. She was excited but also scared, and this wasn't a part of her plans, but she was accepting it anyway.

Amber hugged her also and hung on longer than normal. She wasn't sure what Kerri needed to hear right now, but she said what was on her heart. "That's great, Kerri. You're going to be an awesome mom."

"Thanks," she said. "A little sooner than I was planning, but I guess God knows what He's doing."

The other big news of the day wasn't as shocking as Kerri's. Both she and Seth had been expecting it anytime, but Amber hadn't been thinking about it until Micah and Stephanie announced their engagement when they arrived. The rest of the family already knew, but Micah had wanted to tell his brother in person, so he'd asked the others not to say anything. They were planning to get married next summer after Micah finished his fourth year at OSU. He was planning to go to medical school, but he didn't want to put off marrying Stephanie any longer than that, and Amber was very happy for them.

On the drive back to camp that night, Seth brought up the subject of them having their own children someday, something they hadn't discussed seriously either before they'd gotten married or since. They both wanted to have children, and they had agreed waiting was the most logical choice for them at this point, but how long would they wait? They hadn't discussed that. She told Seth how she honestly felt, and she didn't think his opinion would vary too greatly, but she wanted their decision to be a mutual one.

"If God surprised us like that, I would be okay with it. What else could we do?" She laughed. "But if God is going to guide us in that decision, then I think we have to wait and see when it feels like the right time. Kind of like when we decided to get married. Right now I'm thinking three or four years before we even start trying, but maybe by this time next year or even six months from now I'll feel totally different."

"And I think He'll be faithful to guide us in that," Seth added, taking her hand. "Or surprise us if that's His choice. And I don't want you to ever feel afraid to tell me if that happens, even if you know it's your fault—which isn't the right word, but you know what I mean."

Amber had a mental picture of telling Seth someday she was pregnant, and she knew it would be a very special moment, but she didn't feel ready for that yet. Whenever it happened, she knew it would be the beginning of another big adventure, and she felt grateful she would have a man like Seth to share it with.

Chapter Twenty-Seven

Michaela's final Saturday of the summer was an interesting day. On Wednesday Jake had asked her out, and for some crazy reason she agreed. Maybe because of the quirky way he'd gone about it. She found a camp t-shirt rolled up in her mailbox with the names of all the guys on staff written on the white fabric. There was a note attached that said: *Wash this shirt. Whoever's name is left is the one who wants to take you out this Saturday. If your answer is no, put the shirt in his mailbox by the end of today. If your answer is yes, keep it. (He really hopes it's yes!)*

She'd had a feeling it was Jake before she washed the shirt, and sure enough his name was written in permanent marker to remain very clearly. It made her smile, so she'd given in. Jake could be sweet, but mostly she thought he was a goof-ball who never took anything seriously. After giving him the brush-off all summer, and him being particularly persistent once he'd heard from Nick they were definitely only friends, she had decided to give him the benefit of the doubt. One Saturday with him wasn't going to spoil her summer, she supposed.

The shirt-thing had been silly, but she did see it as a serious effort he was making that had taken thought and planning, and the date turned out to be the same way. He had the entire day planned, but he allowed her to make choices, like where to go for lunch, and whether she wanted to spend the afternoon at the zoo or an amusement park in Portland. He'd driven them there first, not telling her anything, and then revealed his plan once they were eating at a sushi place she liked near her neighborhood.

She'd chosen the zoo because she wasn't in the mood for crazy rides. She felt like the date itself was a crazy enough ride for one day. Then again, going to the zoo was like spending the day with more wild creatures besides Jake, so it was kind of a toss-up. But the zoo had been okay. Just like the drive up to Portland, it had given them a lot of time to talk and get to know each other, something she hadn't really allowed before today—nor had he seemed all that interested in actually knowing anything about her besides the obvious physical things he could see with his own eyes.

He rarely called her by her first name or her camp name. From the first time they'd met back in June, it had been, 'Hey, Beautiful. What Paradise tree did you drop from?' The first time she'd rolled her eyes and walked on by like she would never give him the time of day. But he hadn't taken the hint and kept calling her that until one day during the second week she finally said, 'My name is Michaela. I'd prefer it if you called me that, okay?'

"Okay, beautiful Michaela. Whatever you say."

He'd kept calling her that for a week or two, but then he'd gone back to 'Beautiful' and she hadn't corrected him since. In turn she had started calling him 'Sweetheart', but that had been a mistake. Now if she tried to use his real name, he would correct her and say, 'Hey, that's Jake Sweetheart, Beautiful.'

She stopped talking to him altogether, giving him a patronizing, cordial smile whenever they saw each other, but not saying anything unless he actually asked her a question she felt was worthy of an answer. He had finally taken the hint, and when they'd been at the lake with a bunch of others two weeks ago, he made the effort to have a real conversation with her, and she'd learned a few noteworthy things about him.

He was older than her by a year, and he went to Portland State and the same church as Warner. That's how he had ended up at camp. He'd never worked at a camp before, but he was really enjoying it and seemed somewhat sincere about that. She had talked to him about her mom a little because that had been heavy on her heart that particular day, and he was a good listener.

Jake was well-known by the campers who came each week. By the second day he'd done some crazy thing to get their attention, and it was never the same thing twice, so the counselors thought he was great too. She thought he was cocky and annoying and too full of himself, but whenever she talked about him around Mariah, Mariah would laugh and say, 'Warner used to be the same way,' so she supposed people could change. And she'd seen evidence of another side to him today, but what really blew her away was the path their conversation took during dinner.

He took her to a nice place in downtown Portland. She felt underdressed in her shorts and casual blouse, but apparently they didn't have a dress code because no one said anything, and Jake was dressed even more casually than she was. It was an Indian restaurant, and after they'd ordered their food and he had been more than a little friendly with the waiter who knew his name, she learned his family owned it and they lived upstairs in an apartment. His dad was the head chef, and his mother worked in the kitchen alongside him. Jake had worked here ever since he was fourteen, along with his two older brothers and an older sister.

He'd grown up in India as the youngest son of missionaries, he told her for the first time. His parents had gone there before he was born and had served there for twenty years before returning to the United States. His parents had wanted all of the kids to go to college in the U.S., but they didn't want them to have to return on their own, so they'd made the decision to return as a family, open a restaurant that served Indian cuisine, which they'd learned how to make firsthand during their time there, and put their four kids through college.

"Are they planning to go back?" she asked, completely intrigued by his story now.

"Yes. I'm the last one. My closest brother graduated this year."

"That's really cool," she said. "Your parents doing that for you, I mean."

"Yeah, I didn't think that much of it until about a year ago. It was just our life, you know? But now I can see it was probably a difficult decision for them but a wise one, I think. We're a close family, and we're all in ministry in one form or another, even if we have different career interests. My sister married a doctor and she's a nurse, and they're thinking about going to India in another year or two, maybe when my mom and dad go back."

"How about you? Do you feel God leading you there?"

"Yeah, maybe. But I'm not making any definite plans at this point. I know there are plenty of ministry opportunities and needs right here in America. Two years of college and this summer has proved that to me. I can't believe some of the stories I've heard coming out of those kids' mouths. It's heartbreaking."

They were interrupted by a woman coming to the table then, and Michaela quickly realized it was his mother. Jake introduced them, and she felt honored to meet her. She was a simple woman with her hair pulled back and a sincere smile, and she obviously loved her son. Jake didn't act any different with her, saying some silly thing about the beautiful girl from camp he'd finally managed to get a date with, and Michaela got the distinct impression his mother had heard about her many times. His mother teased Jake about bringing her to meet his family on the first date, and he said something she knew was probably true.

"If I want to impress a girl, I figure my family is my best shot—especially with this one. She's not too appreciative of my other attempts so far. I definitely needed reinforcements to show her I'm not a complete waste of her time."

Their main course plates came then, and his mother had to get back to the kitchen, but she put in a good word for her son before she left. "You are beautiful, Michaela, and I hope we'll be seeing more of you in the future. I keep asking Jake when he's going to bring a girl home for us to meet, and he keeps saying, 'I will when she's the right one.'"

Jake appeared neither embarrassed nor argumentative of his mother's words, as if they were the absolute truth and he wasn't ashamed of them. She felt completely speechless. She couldn't laugh or be disgusted. He started eating, and she began to do the same, but then she stopped.

"Aren't we going to pray first?"

"About what?" he asked.

"Thank God for the food?"

"Thanks, God," he said. "Now eat. This is good stuff."

She did as she was told, and it was very good. She'd had Indian food before, but this was better than anything she'd ever tasted.

"Do you know how to cook like this?" she asked.

"Yep."

"Do you work here full-time?"

"As much as I can. Six days a week usually."

Michaela had to completely rewire her brain about Jake over the Curry Chicken and Vegetables she was eating. Before today if she had to use one word to describe Jake, it would have been, irreverent. Someone with no respect for women, God, basic rules of culture, and anything serious in life.

But in less than a day, he'd proven her completely wrong, and she hadn't even asked him to. She could not have cared less about him making the effort. This day had mostly been about just getting through it. One wasted day out of the summer, and then she would get back to real life:

Things that mattered. People worth her time. Appropriate dialogue and humor. Normal. Sanity. People who played by her rules and fit into her little box of 'goodness'.

"Jake?" she said, taking a sip of her lemon-flavored water and laying her fork down for a moment.

"Yeah, Beautiful?"

"Why didn't you tell me about any of this before?"

"What?"

"Your background, your family, your heart for people?"

"You didn't ask."

"Then why are you doing this? Why don't you hate me and call me a self-centered Barbie Doll?"

"Because you're not. I think you're one of the most beautiful girls I've ever met."

"What do my looks have to do with anything?"

He smiled. "I didn't mean your looks. I meant your heart, Michaela."

She felt like crying. "Is that why you call me Beautiful?"

"It's both. You're beautiful on the outside and the inside. Why did you assume I was only talking about the way you look?"

***

Jessica twirled the diamond ring on her finger and snuggled a little more into Chad. They'd had dinner at the house with her parents and then come into the formal living room to sit and talk, but they were being mostly quiet.

Kerri had called her earlier today and told her about being pregnant. She was thinking about that currently. Initially she had felt shocked and excited for her friend, but it had seemed a little unreal. The reality was hitting her more now, and it made her realize they were all adults now. Married or engaged, having babies, and yet still uncertain about what the future would hold. It made her wonder where she and Chad would be in five years. Married? Most likely. Parents? Maybe. Chad a pastor, herself a teacher like they were planning? Only time would tell, she supposed.

Chad asked her what she was thinking about, and she told him. He'd been different these last few weeks, ever since the night he had given her this ring and told her about his surprise scholarship. God had finally convinced him He had it all under control. No worries. No more doubts. She liked it, but it was taking some getting used to.

"Wherever we are, it's going to be great, sweetheart. Just believe that with me, okay?"

"Okay," she said, not feeling skeptical, just wondering.

"Are you ready to go back to school?" he asked.

"Yes. It's been a really great summer with you and my family, but Lifegate has become like a second home to me, and I miss it."

"Me too," he said.

"You know what else I miss?"

"What?"

"All of our great friends."

"No kidding."

"They're all excited for us."

"Yes," he said.

She knew that was a big deal for him, but it didn't surprise her. If there was one thing she knew about Chad, it was how much his friends admired him and were always behind him one-hundred percent.

And now, as his fiancée, she knew no matter what choices Chad made, or what dreams he chose to follow, or where God led them, she would be his lifetime friend who would always be there for him and be his biggest fan. And she felt very honored to hold such a place in his life.

Chapter Twenty-Eight

The drive back to camp was very different for Michaela than the trip up to Portland had been this morning. Jake had asked her a lot of questions about herself, and she'd answered them, but she had asked very little in return. She already knew all she needed to know or cared about, but she'd been so wrong. And on the way home, she was the one with all the questions.

He was so humble though, it was difficult to keep it serious for long. Jake loved life. He loved to laugh and be happy. He would be serious when he needed to be serious, but today was about having fun after a week of difficult moments with some messed-up guys in his cabin he'd been praying over all week and doing what he could to convince them God's Kingdom was real and something to grab on to and never let go.

He took her to Shari's for a late dessert when they arrived in town near the camp. It was only nine-thirty, and they didn't have to be back until midnight, so they sat there and talked for over an hour, but it was mostly goofiness. He could make anything funny. He could make the waitress laugh, and the teenagers across the aisle, and the old couple in the booth behind him.

She was falling for him, and she knew it, but she didn't know if there was anything she could do about it at this point. The summer was almost over. In two weeks they would be living in different states. Maybe if they both ended up back at camp next year or were both in Portland for the summer they could start something, but it was too late to do anything about it now.

But at least she'd learned a lesson about not judging people so quickly and looking below the surface to a guy's heart before writing him off as an idiot.

On the way out to the car he did something that made it more difficult to avoid the feelings he'd stirred up in her heart, however. He slipped his arm around her waist as if he had complete freedom to do so. He hadn't done anything like that all day, and she would have stepped away and asked him to not touch her if it didn't feel so amazingly good. She'd had kisses that didn't give her goose-bumps like his simple, gentle touch did, and his words didn't help either.

"I've heard a rumor there's a waterfall on the way back to camp. Do you know anything about that, Beautiful?"

She didn't answer, but he waited for one once they reached the car. Instead of opening the door for her, he leaned against it and turned to face her. His arm was completely around her waist, and he was suddenly in her space like he'd never been before, but instead of pushing him away and demanding he never do that again, she looked into his eyes and felt herself smiling.

"Maybe," she said. "What have you heard?"

"I've heard it's a great place to kiss someone. Have you heard that?"

"Yes," she replied.

"Have you ever kissed someone there?"

"No."

"Would you like to?"

She didn't answer that, but he took a chance, leaning forward and speaking words in her ear that made her shiver from head to toe.

"I'd like to kiss you tonight, Michaela. Would that be all right?"

Yes. She wanted to say it, but should she?

He brought his lips in line with hers and stood there motionless for several seconds. She wanted to think about this rationally, but she couldn't. When he spoke, she could feel his warm breath on her lips.

"Would it?" he asked again hopefully, but not like he was expecting anything.

"Yes," she whispered.

"Now or there?"

"Now."

"I'm serious, Beautiful," he warned, giving her one last chance to back out.

"I know."

She closed her eyes. His lips were gentle and sweet. She gave in to the irrational feelings coursing through her whole body. She was afraid he was going to stop before she wanted him to. She wanted to kiss him back more than she was, but she couldn't. He was in control of this kiss, and she wanted him to be. She wanted to be kissed by him, not just kiss him.

"Parking lots are good for kissing too, I guess," he teased her.

"Yes, especially this one."

She felt his lips smile as he kissed her again. "Are you ever serious, Beautiful?"

She couldn't answer because he was kissing her, and she knew she was in so much trouble here. She didn't let guys do this. She didn't fall in love in one day! Jake? Was she out of her mind?

When he stopped kissing her, he leaned his forehead against hers, gently stroked her back, and remained silent for several seconds. He swallowed hard, and she had a fear seize her that he was going to break her heart.

But if he was, it wasn't going to be tonight.

"You're the one I want, Michaela. I'm sorry if that sounds too possessive or whatever. But it's the only way I know how to say it."

"You can say it however you want. Just don't break my heart, okay?"

"I won't, Beautiful. I'm never letting go now."

***

Lauren was having the perfect day with Adam—again. Last Saturday their time at Silver Falls had been perfect like always, followed by dinner and sitting by the river like they were doing again tonight. And even though they'd been separated during the week, it didn't feel like it so much. Not only because they had been meeting in the morning, but also because she'd had a more underlying feeling of connection to him these last two weeks. She could have been all summer, but she'd let silly thoughts creep into her mind about Adam not really missing her and thinking he was getting tired of her and might be looking to move on to someone else.

Since she had gotten her thoughts where they should be—on the reality of his love he showed her all the time—she still missed him, but not always in an 'I can't wait to see him' way. Often she was content to not see him and just believe he was thinking about her and that once they did see each other, it would be the same as always.

But she was looking forward to going back to school, and she felt increasingly so today. Not only because of the time she would have with Adam there, but with her roommates too. She'd gotten to know Colleen better this summer, and she knew she would be a good roommate to have. And she was excited about Emma joining them too. She hadn't gotten to know her well yet, but she had seemed very sweet whenever she'd been around her, and she felt anxious to see how Emma and Tate had fared in their relationship over the summer.

Blake hadn't heard from Tate the last time she'd asked him, so neither of them knew how things were going for him in Iowa. She hoped Emma hadn't missed him too terribly. Not that she wouldn't want them to have the kind of relationship where Emma would miss him while he was away, but she hoped the separation hadn't been too difficult for her. And thinking about it made her temporary separations from Adam seem minor in comparison.

Adam had been quieter today than usual. There was stuff going on at home he was concerned about after getting a letter from his mom yesterday. His sister wasn't doing well, and his mom had asked him to pray for Cassie. She was seventeen and would be a senior this year, but the boyfriend she had and other friends were questionable, and his parents weren't sure she was being truthful about where she was spending her time and what she was doing.

Adam had tried to talk her into working at the camp this summer, but she hadn't wanted to leave her boyfriend back home, and she also planned to go to soccer camp and needed to be back for their opening week of practice that would begin before camp ended. Adam knew it was just an excuse because Cassie was a good enough player to not need soccer camp, and he had been able to get out of soccer practice back when he'd had the same conflict, but Cassie wasn't listening to him or his mom and dad right now.

They had prayed for her together earlier today. Adam hadn't mentioned it since, but she knew he was still thinking about her.

"It's hard to believe it's been a whole year since the first time we did this," Adam said, speaking after several minutes of silence.

"Yes," she agreed. "That was such a surprising day. Even now I can't believe it happened like it did."

He kissed her gently, similar to the first time he had done so. "But I'm glad it did, Angel. My life hasn't been the same since."

"Mine either."

He kissed her for a long time. He'd been kissing her off and on throughout the day, but there was deliberateness in his touch right now that spoke volumes to her about how much he loved her and wanted her in his life. She felt amazed he could show her such passion and have it be completely pure. Like he had no need to do anything more and she could just enjoy the moments of closeness.

When he stopped, he spoke deliberately too, waiting for her to look into his eyes as darkness had begun to fall around them. It was light enough to still see him clearly, and everything about his expression was sincere and truthful. He didn't tell her anything she didn't already know, but he made her believe it a little more.

"I love you, Lauren."

"I love you too."

"Last year I told you I could see us going on to get married someday, and I still feel that way. Do you?"

"Yes."

He smiled, and his simple words would have been enough for her. She hadn't been sitting around, waiting for the day Adam would propose to her. But he had more to say and he took her by surprise, but she wasn't that shocked either.

"I don't have a ring to give you right now, and I'm not sure when I'll be able to afford one, but I need to ask you this anyway. Will you marry me, Lauren? Maybe next summer if we can figure out how to make it work?"

Her answer came easily. "Yes."

"Do you think we can make it work?"

"If God is in this with us, He can make anything work."

"Do you think He's in this?"

She smiled. "I don't see any other explanation. Us getting together the way we did? You having eyes for me over Kerri? And then this year with how He rescued us from disaster?"

She hadn't planned to say that, but now that she had, she continued with her thoughts.

"I didn't know what to do, Adam. It was beyond me, and I just gave it over to God and said, 'If you want us to be together, Jesus, You have to fix this because I don't know how; and He did."

She hadn't told him that before, and she started crying. Her fear of having to let him go had been so great, but she hadn't had to, and this summer he had proved she could trust him again.

He held her for a long time, and she felt safe and loved. She apologized for crying at such a special moment, but he wouldn't hear of it.

"Don't be sorry, Lauren. This is how I always want us to be with each other. Completely real. No hiding our feelings or not saying what's on our hearts. And I'm glad you told me that because it will help define for me how our engagement time should be. That's my promise to you, and with God's help I will keep it."

"I believe you will."

"And I believe we're getting married next summer."

She laughed and joy filled her soul like never before. "Me too, Adam. And I can't wait."

I'd love to hear how God has used
this story to touch your heart.

Write me at:

living_loved@yahoo.com

Additional Titles in the Pure in Heart Series

When I Hear You

When I'm Missing You

When I Follow You

Made in the USA
Middletown, DE
26 November 2018